Worth the Risk

Worth the Risk

A PINE VALLEY NOVEL
Alicia & Jeff

Heather B. Moore

Mirror Press

Interior design by Cora Johnson
Edited by Cassidy Wadsworth Sorenson
Cover design by Rachael Anderson
Cover image credit: Deposit Photos #1927010, Eugena Klykova

Published by Mirror Press, LLC
ISBN-13: 978-1-947152-26-7

PINE VALLEY SERIES

Worth the Risk

Where I Belong

Say You Love Me

Worth the Risk

When Alicia moves back to Pine Valley to help her mom through a serious addiction, the last person she wants to see is her teenage crush, Jeff Finch, who destroyed their friendship in one single disastrous night. But Alicia is determined to not let anything about Jeff affect her, especially since she hasn't seen him in ten years. All she knows is that he's living a successful and charmed life, and she is more than happy to keep anything between them in the past. But when he shows up with a date at the restaurant where she works, Alicia realizes she's still not over her feelings, and Jeff is definitely looking at her in a way he never has before.

One

$\mathcal{A}$licia Waters hid a grimace as she looked up to greet the next patrons walking into the Alpine Lodge restaurant. She'd just read the most recent text from her mom: *You'd better bring home some of that gourmet seafood tonight, and not that soup crap again.*

Her mom was becoming more demanding by the day, it seemed. She hadn't left the house in over two months, and her hoarding had become even worse once she signed up for Amazon Prime. She hadn't even let Alicia throw away the Amazon boxes from all of her online purchases.

"Good evening," Alicia said to the older couple who'd just entered. "Welcome to the Alpine Lodge. Do you have a reservation?" Even though their website and the sign near the doors said *Reservations Required,* it was amazing how many people ignored it.

The man raised his brows, but his brown eyes were warm and friendly. "We don't have reservations, but we're willing to wait." He looked at the woman in a dark purple coat next to him, who must be his wife. "Is that all right, dear?"

"Of course," the woman said, smiling up at her husband.

Alicia liked the couple immediately. They were well dressed, obviously wealthy—as most of the restaurant patrons were at the Alpine Lodge. But unlike so many of the patrons, this couple was friendly.

She hated to disappoint them. "I'm sorry, but we're booked because of the holiday weekend." More specifically, Valentine's Day. She didn't add that the restaurant was usually booked well in advance between Thanksgiving and Valentine's—prime ski vacation season.

"Oh," the woman said, her smile faltering. "I suppose it *is* Valentine's Day for everyone else."

This comment made Alicia curious.

The husband jumped in to explain. "It's our anniversary, and every year, we try a different restaurant." He wrapped his arm about his wife's shoulder. "But I should have called in advance. Knowing this is a small resort town, I guess I didn't think it would be as crowded."

The wife shook her head, but there was a patient smile on her face. "I keep telling him we should just go to lunch, but he's kind of old-fashioned."

The husband chuckled. "No worries. Is there a café in town?"

Alicia blinked and looked from the man to his wife. Instead of becoming upset, they'd been charming. "Let me see what I can do about squeezing you in here," she said. She stepped away from the hostess stand and moved into the restaurant portion to survey the tables.

Just as she remembered, one of the reservations had been changed. A table for six only had four people on it. She signaled Gwen, one of the waitresses, and quickly whispered her idea. Gwen nodded in agreement as she smoothed a strand of her blonde hair that had escaped her messy bun. Alicia and Gwen had struck up a friendship over the past few months, and now more than ever Alicia was grateful. Moments later, she returned to her hostess stand. By now, another couple had entered and was waiting behind the first couple.

"You're in luck." She smiled at the older couple. "We're going to rearrange a couple of things and get you a table ready. It will be about ten minutes. Can I get you anything while you wait?"

The husband grinned, and the wife did a little clap. They really were a sweet couple.

"Thank you, miss," the husband said. "Can we give you a tip?"

"Oh, no," Alicia said with a small laugh, appreciating being called 'miss' instead of 'ma'am'. At the age of twenty-eight, she was well used to the 'ma'am' title. "I'm happy to help, and I hope you have a wonderful anniversary."

Her cell phone buzzed in her pocket, and without looking she knew it was her mom texting again with additional requests.

"Have a seat," she said, waving them toward a long, elegant couch. "I'll let you know when your table is ready." The couple thanked her profusely. But in truth, Alicia was happy to help. She loved the thrill of maneuvering things around and making customers happy. A smile went a long way in her world. She came to work, and people were grateful for her help. She went home, and she could do nothing right.

"Sorry to keep you waiting," Alicia began to say as the next couple walked forward. Her traditional welcome statement stuck in her throat when she saw who had been waiting.

Jeff Finch.

The guy she'd made a huge fool of herself over in high school. The guy who'd burned her in the worst way possible. The guy who'd once been the center of her world. She hadn't seen him face-to-face in more than ten years.

Of all the men to come tonight, when she was working on Valentine's no less, what were the chances?

He was taller than she remembered, but his eyes were the same icy blue. His gaze seemed to bore right into her, and her heart felt like it stopped for a half-second. When it started beating again, it drummed twice as fast. Jeff's hair was also shorter than in high school, and the untamed black curls were mostly disciplined by some type of gel. She didn't remember his shoulders being as broad, but Jeff was a man now, and that probably explained a few things.

She half expected him to say "hi" to her—after all, they'd been neighbors and friends their entire childhood before their fall-out.

But all he said was, "We have a reservation."

The woman standing next to him, who was incidentally holding his hand, looked like she was one of those stock photo models who'd been photoshopped and over-filtered. Perfect makeup, perfect features, perfect hair. The woman's blonde wavy hair was opposite of Alicia's stick-straight brunette hair. And even though Alicia's hostess dress was classy V-neck black, the blonde woman's silver dress seemed to put everyone and everything to shame.

Alicia tore her gaze from the woman and looked back at Jeff. There was no acknowledgment in his eyes, no amusement, and no friendliness.

He didn't recognize her.

Numbness took over Alicia's brain. He had to recognize her; he was just choosing not to. She'd thought she'd put the past behind her, but the hurt was back, and the sharp pain of embarrassment and rejection knotted her stomach. Alicia forced herself to look down at the registrar; she could play his game. "Name, please?"

"Finch," he said. "Jeff Finch. Reservation for two."

The woman said something, but the sound of her voice was merely a blend of sounds compared to the sharp daggers of Jeff's voice.

Alicia blinked, her eyes stinging. *Table fifteen.* There was the name of Jeff Finch right next to it. How did she not see it before now?

Feeling robotic, she grabbed two menus. "This way, please." She turned before she could look into Jeff's eyes again and walked to table fifteen.

She imagined him watching her walk, and she suddenly felt self-conscious in her fitted dress and high heels. But when she stopped at the table and turned, Jeff wasn't looking at her at all. He was checking his phone, his jaw set tightly.

She handed over the menus and told them that their waitress would be with them shortly. Somehow she managed to speak proper English and not stutter. As she walked back to the hostess stand, she wondered why she'd have such a hard time with Jeff Finch, after so long. She should have expected to run into him at some point and was surprised it hadn't been sooner. The thing with small towns is that everyone might move away after high school for a few years, but they usually managed to return.

She should have guessed that Jeff Finch would eventually show up at Alpine Lodge during one of her shifts. He was probably making a lot of money as a realtor in Pine Valley. At least it seemed like it when she'd Googled him from time to time. It wasn't something she was proud of, but during her low moments, she'd Google high school friends to see what was going on in their lives.

Jeff Finch was a realtor in Pine Valley, and with the value of real estate and property sky rocketing the past couple of years, Alicia wouldn't doubt that the suit Jeff wore tonight was quite expensive. The woman at his side was certainly high maintenance.

Gwen showed up. "The table is ready."

"Great, I owe you one," Alicia said.

Gwen smiled. "No problem."

See, everyone is nice to me here, Alicia thought. This was normal. Home was not normal.

Alicia led the older couple to their table and in the process discovered that it was their thirty-eighth anniversary. Once she saw them settled, she couldn't help but glance over at table fifteen.

Her heart about stopped when her gaze connected with Jeff Finch's. He looked away immediately, before she could decide if he was actually watching her, or if it had all been an awkward coincidence. Regardless, heat spread from her neck to her face. She turned and walked briskly to the hostess stand.

Why was she reacting like this? It had been ten years, for heaven's sake. Alicia couldn't technically count Jeff as an ex-boyfriend just because she'd had a huge crush on him their senior year. They'd gone to prom together, and Alicia had obviously read way too much into the invitation. She'd hoped it meant that Jeff liked her as much as she liked him. But all night, he'd had his attention on the new girl in school named Shannon, who was only a junior.

Halfway through the night, Alicia had found them kissing in the hallway when she'd thought he'd taken a bathroom break. She'd been shocked, to say the least.

She hadn't said a word but had called another friend who hadn't gone to prom to come and get her. Jeff could figure out what happened to her on his own. Once at home, she watched out of her window to see him get dropped off after one in the morning by a car she didn't recognize.

By the time school started the next Monday, everyone knew that Jeff and Shannon had hooked up at prom, and they were now an item. Alicia had never talked to Jeff again. Since she knew everything about his schedule and habits and hangouts, it was easy to avoid running into him.

Until now… ten years later.

Alicia exhaled and stared at the list of reservations without reading a word. Why couldn't she forget Jeff and that terrible night? Now, knowing he was somewhere in the restaurant, at table fifteen to be exact, she couldn't seem to slow her drumming pulse no matter how many times she exhaled. Jeff had once been her best friend as well. He wasn't just a random teenage crush. She had allowed herself to hope for so much more.

Alicia blinked back the burning in her eyes as the restaurant doors opened. She greeted the next couple, found their reservation, and led them to their table. This time, she refused to look in the direction of table fifteen.

Two

Jeff didn't need another complication in his life, but from the moment he walked into the Alpine Lodge, he'd been thrown for a loop. If he'd known Alicia Waters worked as the hostess here, he would have made reservations somewhere else. But by the time he'd recognized her as the hostess, it was too late too back out and change his dinner plans with Paige.

Alicia had seated them, with only a quick glance in his direction, then had proceeded to ignore him. Like usual. Two emails chimed on his phone as he sat at the table. He glanced at his phone. Both were from his lawyer, so Jeff pulled them up quickly to scan them. His cousin and former business partner, Kyle, had embezzled money from their real estate company. The lawsuit would be making its first court appearance in a couple of days, and if tonight hadn't been Valentine's, there was no way Jeff would have been out to dinner.

"Is something wrong?" Paige asked.

"Just an email about court on Friday," Jeff said without

looking up. He continued to read through his lawyer's email. *Good.* There was nothing new he needed to know. His lawyer had just sent over copies of both written depositions from Jeff and his former business partner, Kyle.

"Oooh, I wonder if the salmon is good here," Paige continued, reading through the menu aloud. One of her habits, reading the menu to him. Jeff might have found it charming on their first date, but not now.

He and Paige had been dating off and on for a couple of months. Jeff's schedule had been so busy lately that he really didn't have time to date anyone. And Paige was proving to be a time-sap. Which shouldn't be how he felt if he was really interested inFd her. Which he was, mostly, but he was surprised that she had even stuck with him this long. It seemed every date they'd had lately had ended in an argument—about how much time he was spending with her, ironically.

No matter how many times he explained to Paige how much work it took to start up his own real estate business, she didn't seem to understand, or care. She certainly enjoyed the fancy restaurants he could afford, though, and she seemed to ogle over his car more than him. Okay, so buying an exotic car had been a splurge, and he knew it. His one justification was it would keep most of its value if he ever decided to sell. Another justification was that he'd worked his tail off six days a week, and on the seventh day, he wanted to do something fun. Unmarried, and unattached, he'd invested in a Lamborghini, which he couldn't exactly drive in the winter in Pine Valley.

When he'd picked up Paige in his Land Rover tonight, she'd actually pouted.

"I just don't look as good climbing out of a Land Rover as I do your Lamborghini."

Jeff had laughed, but inside he'd been irritated. Paige was

full of comments like that. She didn't see his wealth as a product of late nights and tons of work; she saw it as something that should benefit *her*.

Jeff knew he was in a foul mood. He wasn't looking forward to facing his cousin in court. The lawsuit had dragged on for months, so he should be glad it had finally gotten this far. But when he'd picked up Paige, and she'd made her barbed comments, it hadn't helped. Jeff hadn't been prepared for another complication—that of seeing Alicia Waters at the restaurant.

And she'd looked stunning.

Not the girl next door he'd grown up with, although her hazel eyes were the same, and her pert nose was the same. Okay, her dark hair was the same, but it was sleek and smooth, and longer than it had been in high school. And her figure... well, that had changed the most. She wasn't skinny anymore, but curvy. She still had that birthmark on her wrist that she used to say was an angel kiss. She also wore no ring.

But why should he notice, or even care? She still hated him. He'd seen it in her eyes, even after all these years. How long had it been? Nine? Ten?

Jeff readily admitted that he'd been a jerk in high school. He hadn't thought much with his brain after he turned fifteen, and as a consequence, he'd lost his best friend over some random girl he'd had a crush on for about two weeks. He'd been an idiot at prom, but come Monday morning at school, the gossip had already spread, and there was no way to save face. He was in too deep, and Alicia was intent on avoiding him—as was her right. Their senior year came to an end, and Alicia moved to another city to live with her dad and go to college. He'd seen her pictures with groups of friends on social media, but he never saw any picture that looked like she was in a serious relationship with a guy.

One night he'd even written an email with a long apology, not even sure that her email address was still active, but then he never sent it. He decided that too much time had passed. They'd both moved on, and he thought he could get over the guilt; but apparently it had never truly left.

"Can you shut that thing off?" Paige's voice penetrated his stormy thoughts.

Jeff glanced up. Paige was a beautiful woman, but he'd learned her beauty only went skin deep. "Are you ready to order?" he asked, trying to deflect irritation.

She scoffed. "What does it look like?" Her menu was on the table and her arms folded.

Jeff set down his phone and picked up the menu. He made a pretense of scanning the menu, even though he was no longer hungry. "I think I'll have the braised chicken. What are you having?" It was practically torture to keep his tone light and calm.

"The salmon," she said, her heavily made-up eyes narrowing. "Haven't you listened to a thing I've said?" She reached over and snatched his phone. "I'll keep this until dinner is over."

Jeff stared as Paige slipped his phone into her purse. He didn't react for a moment, because he was so stunned. Yes, he should be more polite and stay off his phone, but he wasn't a twelve-year-old kid either, and this was a crucial week in his career. He was about to let a judge decide if his cousin owed him thousands of dollars. His ears felt hot.

Paige had lifted her chin and was looking at him with a sardonic smile. If he thought she was just teasing him, trying to be funny, he might have laughed. But Paige wasn't a teaser. She wanted his attention on her. All. Of. The. Time.

This was it, he decided. Tonight was the last time he'd see her. Even a guy like him who'd done a lot of idiot things couldn't ditch a date on Valentine's right in the middle of a restaurant. So, he reached for the ice water that had been brought at some point and drank half of it down.

"That's better," Paige crooned, propping her elbows on the table. "You work too much, sweetie. We should go on a vacation. Someplace where there's no cell service."

Jeff rubbed the back of his neck, hard, hoping the pressure would keep his temper down. "My busy season starts in about three weeks," he ground out.

"Perfect." Paige waved her hand, flashing her fake sparkly nails. "We could spend a week in Hawaii. Or . . ." Her already big eyes grew bigger. "Italy. I've always wanted to go there. And since you like Italian cars, it will be perfect."

Fortunately, their waitress showed up just then to take their orders.

"Wow," Paige said, when the waitress left. "Gwen sure checked you out."

He frowned. "Who's Gwen?"

"The waitress," Paige said. "She was practically all over you."

"What are you talking about?" he asked. The waitress had taken their order and left. She might have smiled at him, but that was standard, right? He could only remember that she had blonde hair twisted into some sort of messy bun, but didn't remember much else, let alone her name.

"You can't tell me you didn't notice her staring at you like she wanted to have you for *her* dinner," Paige pressed. "She's probably one of your ex-girlfriends. You've got like eight in this town."

Jeff and Paige had confessed all about their exes on their second date when too much wine had been involved. He more than regretted it now. But instead of snapping back like he wanted to, he exhaled slowly. "I didn't notice the waitress. I don't know her, and she's not my ex. Pine Valley is a small town, but it's been growing like crazy the past couple of years. There are a lot of new faces here. You can't assume that every woman who gives me a second look was someone I dated."

Paige pushed her lower lip out like a small child might when not getting the ice cream she wanted. Jeff was seriously questioning his judgment in women. His dating life had been a disaster for the most part. Once things went beyond the first few dates, Jeff found that he wasn't up to the task of being in an actual relationship.

"You're so mean sometimes," Paige said, her pout still apparent for everyone in the restaurant to see if they cared to pay attention.

Mean? How was he being mean now? Oh, he could tell her stories, but he'd refrain. "I'm not trying to be mean," he said, glancing around the restaurant, wondering if he could signal the waitress to put in a rush on their meal. Then he caught sight of *her*. Alicia was escorting another couple to their table. She'd always been tall, but her legs were a mile long in those heels of hers.

Before he could tear his gaze away, she looked over at him, and their eyes connected.

Jeff quickly refocused his attention on Paige, who was, thankfully, looking down at *her* phone. Ironic. Then he noticed that her brow was furrowed.

"Is something wrong?" It was his turn to ask. He sort of hoped there was something wrong—not too serious of course, but just enough to cut their date short.

"My call time was moved up to 7:00 am tomorrow," she said.

Jeff waited.

She looked up, her pouty face in full force. "That means

I need to go home early. I can't have bags under my eyes for the photoshoot. My agent will kill me."

Jeff nodded. "We don't have to go to the movie. I'll take you home after dinner."

She didn't react for a moment. Then she smiled. "All right."

And just like that, her mood was better, and she stopped picking on him. The food arrived, and the rest of the meal went better than he expected. Paige talked about the upcoming photoshoot most of the time, and Jeff was more than happy to let her carry most of the conversation.

He saw Alicia come into the main restaurant twice more—at least, that was the number of times he allowed himself to look up when she entered the room.

"Do you want dessert?" he asked Paige, even though he knew the answer would be no. Models didn't eat dessert.

"Hardly," she said, her tone soft. She always became a nicer person after a meal. "Let's go. I should probably change my nail color too. No sparkles." Another pout.

Jeff slipped a hundred-dollar bill into the bill fold the waitress had brought. He was thankful he'd brought cash and didn't have to wait for a credit card to be processed. He stood, then helped pull back Paige's chair as she rose. He helped her into her jacket and led the way out of the restaurant.

As they neared the hostess stand, Jeff saw that Alicia stood there, and no one was waiting to be seated.

It would be rude to walk past without thanking her, and Jeff knew from experience that Paige wouldn't be the one to speak up.

"Our compliments to the chef," Jeff said as they walked past the hostess stand.

Alicia looked up from where she'd been texting someone on her phone. Her eyes settled on him, and Jeff wished that

Paige wasn't with him—that he could form a coherent apology, even though it was ten years overdue.

"I'll let him know," Alicia said with a smile.

The smile wasn't for him, and Jeff knew it. Her smile was a hostess's smile, one she likely gave dozens of times a night. But it still made his guilt wedge even deeper as the memories of her smiling assailed him. When they'd been friends. When he hadn't broken her heart yet.

Three

Jeff had spoken directly to her. He hadn't said her name; he hadn't acted like he knew her other than as a patron speaking to a hostess at a restaurant; but Alicia *knew*. She knew he had recognized her. The glances she caught from him at the restaurant had been enough proof. As she drove home from the restaurant through the dark night, her mind and heart buzzed with memories.

It was nearly 11:00 p.m. when she pulled into the cracked driveway of her mom's home. Most of the lights were still on in the house, which meant her mom was still awake, waiting and hungry. Alicia gathered up the take-out boxes and climbed out of her car.

She tried to talk herself into a pleasant mood, even though she was exhausted. Now wasn't the time to feel sorry for herself and regret all the things she'd given up to move back home. She had a college degree in marketing and had been working for a surf shop chain. Even though they'd said they could hold the job for her, she didn't think it was fair to make them do that. She didn't know how long she'd be in Pine Valley.

So, she'd paid an extra month's rent to her roommate Josi and told her to find a new roommate. There hadn't been a boyfriend to leave. She and David had broken up right after Christmas last year, and all her dates with other men after that had been one-time dinners. Alicia knew it was because David had cheated on her, and she had trust issues to overcome. Since moving to Pine Valley, the last thing on her mind was dating.

Alicia found her mom at the kitchen table with her paper plate, plastic fork, and knife set out. Only about a third of the table was usable—just enough room for two people to sit and eat. The rest of the table was stacked with old magazines and boxes of picture frames.

"Hi, Mom," Alicia said in a cheerful tone.

Her mom said nothing, just stood with her hands on her hips as she watched Alicia set down the bag and take out the boxes. Her mom shared the same hair color with Alicia, although hers now had plenty of gray strands in it. At age fifty-nine, Lila Waters was a ghost of who she'd been before. Her thinness was nearly skeletal, her skin pale from rarely going outside.

"I have spinach ravioli and salmon," Alicia continued. Her mom's silences were worse than her yelling. "I also brought a can of soda, although you might not want that much sugar this late at night." She stepped back from the table.

Her mom sat down, pulling her ratty bathrobe about her. Even though she had four or five newer ones stuffed in her closet, she insisted on wearing her old blue floral one day after day.

When Alicia tried to sneak and wash her mom's things in the middle of the night, her mom would throw a major fit the next day. Alicia moved back from the table as her mom started to eat. Then she quietly went about her routine, turning off lights and locking doors. If her mom was left to her own devices, she'd keep all the lights on throughout the night. It seemed that even though Alicia had been later than usual, her mom was in a calm mood.

But Alicia knew better than to bring up anything that would distress her mom, so she didn't remind her that tomorrow the social worker would be coming to the house. It wasn't as if her mom would let Alicia clean up the place anyway. Any throwing away that Alicia did had to be done when her mom was asleep, and Alicia had to make it look like nothing was missing.

Now, Alicia walked down the hall, lined with stacked boxes, some of them unopened. They contained her mom's latest purchases, which were probably fuzzy blankets—her mom's newest fetish. Yes, it was cold outside, and Pine Valley had seen a decent snowfall this season, but the heater worked fine, and they already had plenty of blankets.

Alicia unlocked the door to the back bedroom that she'd lived in as a child, and more recently when she moved home in the summer after her mom's run in with the law. Alicia had to keep her mom out of her room somehow, or things would go missing, or even worse, end up stacked in here too. In contrast to the rest of the house, Alicia's room was sparse. A twin bed, a single side table, a scuffed desk, a small closet with her clothes and shoes. A bookshelf full of her childhood stuffed animals and mementos . . . things from when her life was normal. When Jeff was her best friend. When her parents were still married. When her mom hadn't been a hoarding recluse.

Changing her clothes into her winter pajamas, which amounted to yoga pants and a long-sleeved T-shirt, Alicia thought about how her life used to be so simple. How she used to be happy and how routine her days were. She turned off her light and climbed into the cold covers. Her body heat would warm them up in a few moments, but she shivered as she waited. The sounds of the house were quiet, which meant that her mom had gone to bed without incident.

Alicia reached for her cell and double-checked that her alarm was set for 4:30 a.m., when she'd get up and clean her mom's dinner mess. She'd also find other things to throw away. Then she'd sneak out of the house with the garbage bag and walk it to one of the neighbor's trash cans, or better yet, find a public dumpster. If she deposited any garbage in their own trash bin, her mom would just pull it out.

Alicia exhaled. How had her mom become like this? Alicia had done some research on hoarders and discovered that they usually started hoarding, or getting worse, when they experienced a great loss. Had the loss been her parents' divorce? Or had the loss been when Alicia had chosen her dad over her mom? It wasn't really choosing. Alicia had graduated high school, lived and worked at home for a few months. Her mom had become more and more lazy, skipping work, rarely cleaning, and not spending time with friends anymore. At first Alicia thought maybe her mom was depressed, and they even went to the doctor together to get a prescription for anti-depressants.

But her mom's moods were even more bizarre on the medication, and she never got a refill. Since her mom was getting alimony from her dad, Alicia hadn't completely worried about her mom missing work, but worried more for her mental health. Not only did her mom isolate herself, but she wanted to isolate Alicia too.

At nineteen, Alicia had determined that she wasn't going be trapped in her mom's house, and so she decided to go to college near her dad's home in Sacramento. The visits back home to her mom's had become shorter and more unbearable. The hoarding had become more obvious after Alicia had been gone a while, since it had started to spread to the rest of the house.

When social services called her last summer and told her that her mom had been cited for taking garbage out of the neighbors' trash bins, Alicia had come home to meet with the social worker. She was told, point blank, that if her mom trespassed again, she could be looking at jail time. It was then that Alicia decided to move back home to see if she could get her mom some help. But as the weeks went by, it was clear that the best way to keep peace was to let her mom go about her hoarding and for Alicia to get rid of stuff on the sly.

Alicia took her mom to therapy once a week, but even that tapered off when her mom refused to leave the house. The therapy appointments were reduced to phone conversations in which her mom did little talking at all. Alicia's only escape from her mom was her job, and the occasional night out with Gwen. Whenever she ran into anyone from high school, Alicia just pretended things were great and that she was helping her mom, who was sick. She never went into the true details of her mom's condition.

Closing her eyes, Alicia tried to relax and let her mind drift off, away from issues with her mom and away from the memories of Jeff Finch. She needed to sleep, and she was exhausted, so why would her thoughts not fade? Seeing Jeff with a date at the restaurant should have been no big deal. Ten years was a long time to still be affected by him. He'd looked older, but in a good way. More serious, more mature, more . . . everything. His family had sold their house years ago, his parents moving to some fancy retirement place, and Jeff lived who knew where—probably in one of the new subdivisions at the base of the mountain. Wherever he lived, was no concern to her. So what if he was single? She didn't need to analyze why; he was obviously living the bachelor lifestyle and dating gorgeous women.

If social media could be relied on, it meant Jeff Finch was definitely out of her league. She'd seen pictures of his Lamborghini, and it hadn't been hard to miss the many pictures of him with his rich clients and beautiful dates. Here Alicia was, living in her childhood bedroom, in the middle of squalor. She blew out a frustrated breath. Hopefully by the morning she'd forget how great Jeff looked in his suit and how beautiful his date was. And how everyone seemed to have a better and happier life than she did.

Four

Jeff sat in his Land Rover outside of his childhood home. He couldn't sleep, and now it was four o'clock in the morning. So he'd given up and started his day, which led to putting together real estate comps for some of his clients. When he'd finished a few, he'd decided to go for a drive and ended up here, in his old neighborhood.

Earlier that night, he'd dropped off a pouty Paige, who was worried that she'd eaten too much at dinner and would be bloated for her photoshoot. When Jeff asked if it was a swimsuit shoot, she'd glared at him and told him it was for a sunglass company and only her head would be showing, but bloating could be seen in a person's cheeks.

Who knew?

Jeff couldn't drop her off fast enough. He'd walked her to the door, and when she'd invited him in, he reminded her that she had to get up early. He gave her a quick hug, but no kiss. If she noticed how distant he was being, she didn't pick up on it. He'd wanted to break things off then and there, but he wasn't sure if she was a crier. And what if she cried? And then her eyes became puffy and ruined her photoshoot? He didn't know much about bloating, but he knew a little about puffiness.

So he'd left her without breaking things off, though he was determined that the next time they spoke, he'd tell her. It would have to be soon. Later today, probably. He'd learned his lesson well with Alicia. And he'd prided himself in being more upfront with the women he dated. If he didn't see it going anywhere beyond a few dates, then why drag it out?

So why was he sitting in his Land Rover, across the street from his old house, in the middle of the night? A quick search on the MLS real estate system told him that the house had been through three owners since his parents had retired and moved. Another search told him that Alicia's mom, Lila Waters, was still the listed homeowner on the house next door. And there were lights on.

It was nearly 4:30 a.m., and Jeff wondered if Lila Waters was an early riser, or perhaps a night owl. Then he noticed the car in the driveway and the sticker in the back window that said *CSU—Sacramento*. Some parents were proud and put stickers on their cars of their kids' colleges, but something told Jeff this wasn't the case. The car belonged to Alicia. It was a newer model Honda Accord, and although it was an average car, it stuck out in this neighborhood. While some neighborhoods in Pine Valley were extravagant, this neighborhood hadn't changed in decades. Most of the people who lived here were lower class. Husband and wife both worked, aging in-laws lived with them, and their cars were older models.

Jeff kept apprised of these types of demographics so he could better serve his real estate clients. Finding the right comps and getting the most value out of a house were what made his deals successful. Like any real estate agent, he was a slave to the market, so it was imperative that he find every advantage possible. Whether it was to highlight a nearby park, or the friendliness of the neighbors, or the low crime rate, or the closeness of the ski resort . . . it was all part of the sales pitch.

The air in the Land Rover had grown cold enough to start bothering him, and he'd been here a while, so he reached to turn on the ignition when someone came out the front door of the Waters' house. Jeff paused to watch, not wanting to start the ignition while the woman was outside. Yet, she didn't walk like the sixty-something woman Lila Waters would be.

No, this woman's dark hair was illuminated by the porch light and swung about her shoulders as she hurried down the porch steps. *Alicia?* Jeff stared as she continued her swift strides toward the Honda and unlocked the trunk, then stuffed a large garbage bag inside. She jumped in the driver's seat and started the car. The brake lights glowed, and she backed out of the driveway. Where was she going at 4:30 in the morning?

Without thinking about what he was doing, Jeff started his engine and pulled out behind the Honda. Not too close so that she became suspicious. It was quite easy to follow her at a distance, since there were no other cars on the streets. Her taillights were the only thing to keep track of.

Jeff slowed again when she exited the neighborhood and pulled into a gas station that was closed. Was she getting gas? Pine Valley had yet to adopt an all-night gas station. He pulled to a stop at the curb about one hundred yards away and turned off his engine and lights. The interior dome lights came on, and he scrambled to switch them off manually. Finally, in the darkness, he watched Alicia park by a dumpster, then climb out of her car. She popped open the truck and lugged the garbage sack out, then dumped it into the trash.

She stood there for a moment, as if she was rethinking her plan of throwing away a large amount of trash so early in the morning. Then she turned back to her car. Her actions were no longer quick, but slow, as if she was tired. She couldn't have gotten much sleep between her shift at the restaurant and now. Or maybe she hadn't gone to sleep at all.

Jeff wasn't exactly sure why he was spying on Alicia Waters, especially after all these years. Despite the fact that she'd developed into a gorgeous woman and seemed more *real* compared to Paige, he had no right to follow Alicia this way. He really knew nothing substantial about her. Social media wasn't an accurate depiction of anyone's life; he knew that better than anyone.

Alicia shut the trunk of her car, climbed in, and pulled out of the gas station. He slid down in his seat as she turned onto the road and drove right past him. He doubted she'd seen him, especially with his tinted windows. But he'd definitely seen *her.* And memories surfaced about their childhood, their friendship, and how they'd confided in each other until he was an idiot and destroyed everything between them. Even her walk was familiar, the tilt of her head when she was speaking with the restaurant patrons, the habit she still had of tucking her hair behind her left ear. Some things about her had changed, though. He'd had time to observe her when she was speaking to the older couple at the restaurant. Her voice was deeper, smoother, her cheekbones more defined, and she hadn't been wearing a ring.

Of course, he knew she wasn't married. There would have certainly been something on social media if she had. But no ring also told him there was no fiancé either. And something about that made him happy. Jeff didn't let himself analyze why he was happy about that, and he started the engine and drove to his office on Main Street. He might be two hours earlier than usual, but he'd be surrounded by plenty of work at his office, and it would distract him.

Jeff parked in the back of the row of Main Street buildings. He climbed out of the Land Rover and was immediately greeted by a pitiful meow. A few weeks ago, a stray calico cat had shown up in the parking lot, searching for scraps of food. Jeff's receptionist, Clara, had felt sorry for it, bought a bag of cat food, and begun leaving a bowl at the back door of the office. So now the cat had expectations, although it still wouldn't let Jeff touch it.

"All right, all right," he told the cat. "I'll get you something."

He unlocked the back door while the cat walked in little circles, as if it couldn't stand the wait. Jeff poured some cat food into the metal bowl, and the cat pretty much attacked it, eating and purring at the same time.

"I guess purring is how you say thank you?" Jeff said. "Well, you're welcome."

He pulled the door shut and left the cat to its blissful meal. Then he turned on the rest of the lights in the office. It would be a full hour before the corner café opened and he could get a couple of muffins. For now, he settled for making instant coffee. He couldn't remember when he'd last stayed awake all night. Well, he could remember—it actually was his senior prom.

Jeff groaned and shook his head. Would he ever be able to completely forget about that night? Would he be able to forget the look on Alicia's face when he'd heard her enter the hallway and he looked up from kissing Shannon? Jeff had been a hormonal teenager, and even though he had no problem with Alicia's looks, it always felt like she was off-limits because they were best friends. They'd even talked about their crushes and dates.

He remembered when he told Alicia about his first kiss, and how she'd laughed and blushed, then asked a million questions. Alicia had never told him about her first kiss—and now he wondered if she'd kissed anyone in high school.

Shannon had been flirting with him for weeks, and all of his friends had agreed she was hot. So at prom when she came up and talked to him when Alicia was talking to some other friends, he acted his normal, friendly self. Yes, he was interested, but he also wasn't prepared when Shannon had whispered in his ear, "I have something to show you in the hallway."

Like an idiot, he'd fallen for the line and met her in the hallway a few minutes later. She kissed him first, yes, but he also kissed her back. And then to save face, he kept dating her for a few more weeks. But what he didn't realize then was that by saving face around his friends, he'd lost his best friend.

Alicia never spoke to him again.

Jeff powered on the office laptop and sipped at his nuked coffee as he opened Facebook. He shouldn't . . . but he did. He typed in Alicia's name and watched her profile load. She'd posted about a week ago—a picture of her and another woman who looked vaguely familiar. They were standing in front of a homeless shelter—which had to be in another city, since there wasn't one in Pine Valley—and the caption said, "Spending my day off with Gwen."

Gwen. Jeff gazed at the blonde woman next to Alicia. He clicked on her name and was taken to Gwen's profile. *Ah.* She worked at Alpine Lodge, and she was the waitress who had served him last night. The one Paige had been upset about—if only she knew it was the hostess he actually had a history with.

Jeff scrolled through Gwen's pictures, seeing that she must spend most of her time off working at that particular homeless shelter. Needless to say, he was impressed. If Gwen was a waitress, she was probably just getting by herself, and she seemed like a selfless person. And a good friend to Alicia. For some reason, that made Jeff feel better, and perhaps less guilty for being such a lousy friend ten years ago. It seemed that Alicia had moved on, had good friends, was back in her hometown, and was most likely happy. She'd looked incredible—wasn't that a good indicator?

Still curious, Jeff returned to her page and scrolled through her posts and pictures. He was interested about one thing. Why would a college graduate want to work as a hostess at a restaurant, even a posh one, and live at home in a run-down neighborhood? He wondered what her Facebook profile wasn't showing. What heartaches might lurk beneath her smiling face and breezy posts. He found one picture of her with her dad—it looked like they were at some sort of Christmas party from a few years back. There were no pictures of her mom, and a search for Lila Waters brought up no hits.

Jeff sat back in his chair and scrubbed a hand through his hair. He felt drained. But he knew even if he took the morning off and went home to sleep, he'd never be able to sleep. So he did something he didn't think he'd do in a million years. He sent a Facebook friend request to Alicia Waters.

Five

"What have you done?" a woman screamed through Alicia's bedroom door while simultaneously pounding on it.

Alicia groaned. She hadn't meant to fall back asleep, and now the winter sun was high in the sky. "Hang on, Mom," she called back, her throat still scratchy with sleep.

"You threw away my blue hot pads, didn't you?" her mom shrieked.

Alicia felt ill. She'd thrown away the food-crusted, half-burned hot pads weeks ago, hoping that the other dozen or so sets that her mom kept around would mask the missing blue ones. Apparently not.

Alicia nearly stumbled when her foot caught on the edge of the small area rug in her room. She unlocked and opened the door to face her mom's reddened face.

"Those hot pads were a wedding gift!" her mom said, not yelling quite as loud, but her voice still had plenty of power. "They were from Aunt Irma, who knitted them herself."

"I'll help you find them," Alicia said. "Have you checked all the drawers in the kitchen?" She was lying to her mom, but she had to talk her off the ledge and get her calmed down before she told her the truth. Today might require an emergency therapy session.

Her mom's voice was calmer when she said, "I looked everywhere."

"Okay, I'll start looking too." Alicia led the way down the hall and walked into the kitchen. The place was a disaster—more so than usual. In addition to the stacks of clutter, every drawer was open, and kitchen towels, ketchup packets, bread bag ties, and various colored hot pads were scattered about the floor. There was also a very distinct smell of something burning in the oven.

Alicia flew to the stove top and turned off the oven. "What are you cooking?" she asked as she opened the oven door. Black smoke poured out, and Alicia waved it away so she could peer inside.

"I'm making cookies—is that a crime now?" her mom said.

Burned lumps on the cookie sheet were all that were left of her mom's creation. Alicia grabbed a hot pad from the floor and pulled out the cookie sheet. Then she moved past her scowling mom and opened the front door. Alicia set the burned pan with the black cookies on the front porch.

She hurried to open the kitchen windows, even though it was cold outside, while her mom stood and watched, her eyes narrowed.

"We don't want the smoke detector to go off," Alicia said, as if she needed to explain this to her mom.

"They won't go off because I disabled them," her mom snapped.

"Why did you do that?" Alicia folded her own arms. There were some things that were just plain unsafe, and not having working smoke detectors was one of them.

"The chirping drives me crazy!"

Alicia wanted to laugh, a crazy laugh. Her *mom* was driving her crazy. "The chirping sounds means you have to change the batteries."

"I know," her mom said. "But one of them kept doing it even after I changed the battery."

Alicia blinked. "Then it probably just needs to be completely replaced. How long have the smoke detectors been disabled?"

Her mom shrugged and turned away. All of the yelling must have drained her, because instead of continuing her search for the blue hot pads, she sat at the table and propped her elbows on a stack of grocery coupons that she religiously cut and saved but never used.

When her mom was quiet and pensive like this, Alicia found that she felt a lot more compassion for her. She wished her mom could have a normal life, that her phobias and anxieties didn't keep her home-bound. That she could garden, walk around the neighborhood, go to a mother-daughter lunch.

Alicia took a deep breath and sat in the other chair at the table. "Those blue hot pads were so damaged that they couldn't even be washed," she started. "And I'm sorry that I didn't know they were a wedding present. When I moved in, I didn't think they were usable anymore, and you had so many others I didn't think to ask you about them. I'm sorry I didn't ask."

Her mother didn't react for a moment. This was actually a good thing. In therapy, they'd both been told to listen to each other, then take a moment before replying. Alicia had also learned to not call her mother's things "clutter" or "garbage" but to understand that they were valuable to her mom.

Alicia was also supposed to ask permission before throwing anything away—but until the therapist saw the actual state of their house, Alicia had to take some things into her own hands. Her mother had *never* given her permission to throw anything away, and every request turned into a major argument. Thus, Alicia's early morning forays to a dumpster.

Her mother finally lifted her head, and it tore at Alicia's heart to see the tears. Yet, on the other hand, their therapist had told her that tears were good—it meant that her mom was allowing herself to feel emotion instead of covering it up with more hoarding. "Blue's my favorite color."

The statement surprised Alicia—not that her mom's favorite color was blue but that she wasn't demanding to search a dumpster to get back the hot pads.

She swallowed back her relief, then did something she'd sworn never to do. "What if we look up blue hot pads on Amazon? See if there's any you like."

Her mom's eyes immediately brightened, making Alicia feel even more guilty. She was totally playing on her mom's weaknesses to deflect the guilt from herself. But sometimes, a girl just needed a break.

While her mom browsed Amazon and undoubtedly ordered more things than just blue hot pads, Alicia quietly cleaned up the floor. Her mom didn't even say anything when Alicia brought out the broom and mop and scrubbed it clean. Perhaps they'd reached some sort of truce. Although it pained Alicia to put all the hot pads back into the drawers. Several of them were in no better condition than the blue ones had been.

Next, Alicia retrieved the pan of burnt cookies from the front porch. It gave her a few moments to stand in the cold air and breath it in. It was a beautiful, cold afternoon, and the layer of snow on the lawn had frozen. As a kid, she used to love to try and balance on frozen snow. Invariably, her boots would crack through, and Jeff would laugh at her.

Jeff. His laugh.

She shook her head, dispelling the memory. A car drove by, and someone waved. Alicia couldn't see who it was, but she waved back—it was sort of a tradition in these types of neighborhoods. People waved to each other. Alicia had been gone for a long time and hadn't kept up with all the new move-ins, but she did know that the Finch house had seen people come and go. She glanced over at the yard and noted that it was its usual pristine self. Even in the dead of winter, the bushes looked neatly trimmed, and the two pine trees held an elegant dusting of snow on their branches, making it look like a postcard house. The driveway and sidewalk were clear and completely free of ice. Alicia could almost picture Mr. Finch outside, methodical in his yard work no matter what time of year. And Mrs. Finch . . . she was one of those moms who baked cookies after school.

Speaking of cookies. Alicia looked down at the burnt mess she was holding as tears pricked her eyes. She was being ridiculous, of course. No one's life was perfect, not even the Finches. But right now, anything sounded better than the situation Alicia was in.

She sniffled and wiped at her eyes, knowing she was just tired. Sleeping four hours hadn't really been enough, although she'd survived it plenty of times. She wanted to call her dad and lay it all out on him, but she already knew what he would say. He'd tell her to let her mom figure things out on her own, that if she got arrested, then she got arrested. He'd tell her to move out and to get her own place.

But the problem was, Alicia couldn't leave her mom alone. Her mom had literally no one. And she couldn't imagine that jail would help her mom at all—and then what? Would her mother become a permanent resident of a psych ward somewhere? Alicia squeezed her eyes shut, and not sure if she was saying some sort of prayer or not, she pleaded to find a way to help her mother. The therapy had helped, but it wasn't enough. And Alicia didn't know how much longer she could live here.

She wiped at the tears again and inhaled sharply. She couldn't go back inside crying. Finally, feeling calm again, she entered the house. Her mother was still on the computer, so Alicia started to scrape off the burnt mess into the sink. She scrubbed the baking sheet clean and dried it. After putting it away, she glanced over at her mom, who was in her own little world, a crooked smile on her face. Alicia scanned her mom's ratty bathrobe, her unwashed hair—another battle Alicia had fought and lost—the way her mom's skinny foot tapped at the floor.

And suddenly the tears were back. Alicia hurried from the room and walked to her bedroom, where she changed her clothing. She'd go for a long, cold walk and clear her head. Then she'd take a nap before work.

When she returned to the kitchen, she told her mom, "I'm going on a walk. You can call my phone if you need anything."

Her mom barely looked up, then refocused on the computer.

All right, then. Alicia left the house, locking the door behind her. She set off down the neighborhood and ignored the childhood memories that flooded through her as she passed landmarks that had connections to Jeff Finch. She'd been fine in this neighborhood for months, but seeing him last night must have triggered everything. It was probably why she was so emotional today.

She wished she could call Gwen and dump everything on her, but the nice thing about Gwen was that Alicia hadn't told her about her mom. So it meant that time with Gwen was like a break from worrying or talking about her mom. Alicia could separate herself from all of that and just have a good time with her friend.

She kept her pace brisk and turned the corner. The next neighborhood was as old as hers, but many of the residents had done major remodels on their homes, so the prices were much higher. A couple of the houses were for sale, which surprised her. Usually houses didn't go on the market until spring.

She continued walking. Across the street about another block down, a young couple came out of one of the for-sale homes. Another man was with them. They seemed to be in an animated conversation over something, and Alicia decided they were potential home buyers with their realtor.

Then she nearly stumbled on a sidewalk crack she hadn't been paying attention to. The single man—the realtor—was Jeff Finch, and he'd just seen her too.

Six

Jeff squinted against the winter sun as a movement caught the corner of his eye. He glanced over, prepared to give a friendly wave to a neighbor, hoping the neighbor would stop and tell Mr. and Mrs. Jensen how great this area was. But the woman didn't wave. In fact, she looked quickly away the moment their gazes connected.

Jeff's breath caught. It was Alicia. Her hair might be mostly concealed by a purple beanie hat, and her turned-up collar prevented him from seeing her entire face, but he'd gotten a good-enough look.

He wondered if she was training for a race-walking competition, or if she was just trying to get out of speaking to him. Probably the latter.

"You have my number," Jeff said to Mr. and Mrs. Jensen. "I've got to catch up with someone and ask a few questions . . . about the neighborhood. Please let me know your thoughts after you discuss this home. We have two others lined up tomorrow to visit."

"Will do. Thanks, Jeff," Mr. Jensen said.

Jeff shook both of their hands, then strode down the walkway to the sidewalk. Alicia was about a hundred yards away now, still walking fast. He hadn't checked Facebook since he'd sent the friend request, and now he pretty much knew she'd deny it. So the only way to contact her was to speak to her in person. Jeff increased his stride, and when it was clear he wouldn't be able to catch up with her without breaking into an all-out run, he called out, "Alicia?"

Her step hitched. She'd heard him, but she didn't slow or turnaround.

"Alicia," he called again, looking about to make sure nosy neighbors weren't staring at him. When she still didn't slow down or turn, he said, "I know you probably don't want to talk to me, but if you could just give me thirty seconds, then I won't bother you again."

She continued to walk, but her step was noticeably slower, and Jeff quickly gained ground.

Finally, she came to a stop, still not looking at him. Jeff was relieved, but his pulse was also drumming with nervousness. When he caught up with her, she turned to face him.

Her hazel eyes stared up at him, and the first thing he noticed was that she'd been crying.

His heart twisted. "I'm sorry," he blurted out. "I'm sorry for acting like I didn't know you last night. I'm sorry for not apologizing after prom. I'm sorry for what happened with Shannon, and for not—"

"Stop," Alicia said, holding up her hand.

Jeff stopped.

She took a deep breath and blinked a couple of times. The purple color of her beanie made her hazel eyes look more green. It also brought out the pink in her cheeks—or maybe it was the cold bite in the air. "It's been ten years, Jeff. I'm fine." She motioned toward him with her hand. "And you're obviously fine." She shrugged in a small, resigned way. "Life goes on. We were teenagers—kids, really—and emotions and hormones were crazy back then."

Jeff nodded, relieved she was saying all of this. That she was basically accepting his apology. But the guilt was still a hard thing in his stomach. "Can I make it up to you some-how?" he asked, his thoughts racing way ahead of his speech. "Name it, and I'll do it. I can't stand knowing that I've made you cry."

Her eyes widened. "You think I'm crying about *you*?"

"I—I can tell you've been crying," he said. "And when you practically sprinted away from me, I just thought . . ."

She laughed, but it wasn't a warm laugh. "Wow. You've still got your ego, I see." She took a step back, shaking her head.

Panic shot through Jeff. He was going to lose her, here and now, he felt it. "Wait," he said, reaching out and grasping her arm. As quickly as he touched her, he released her. "I mean, if you're not crying about . . . me . . . what's wrong?"

Her brows shot up, telling him that he'd crossed a line. Her personal life wasn't his business. He knew it, she knew it, but he couldn't seem to stop himself. "Can I help you with something? I'll do whatever you need. Is it money?"

At least she wasn't turning and walking away again, but the expression on her face told him that he was pretty much the idiot he was ten years ago. "You think you can help me? Fix my problems?" She scoffed. "That's really arrogant, Jeff. I'm not some damsel in distress you can throw money at and come away smelling the hero. Not every problem in this world is about money."

He raised his hands. "I know. I just—"

"You feel guilty, that's all this is." Her eyes flashed with fire. "You don't care about *me*, and I don't know if you ever really did. Best friends don't break each other's hearts."

Jeff looked away. It was hard to see the raw pain in her eyes. "I did care about you, Alicia," he said in a quiet voice, meeting her gaze again. "I was mortified about what I did, and I was an idiot for trying to be someone I wasn't."

"Yeah," she said with another shrug. "I get it, peer pressure." Her gaze dropped. "I can take care of myself, thank you."

"I know," Jeff said. "I shouldn't have suggested . . . well, I shouldn't have assumed anything. I mean, I have no right to." Their gazes held for a long moment.

And then her face crumpled.

Before she could turn away and hide her tears, Jeff pulled her into his arms. She was stiff at first, but as her shoulders shook from crying, she melted against him and buried her face against his neck. Whatever her pain and heartbreak were, it traveled straight to his own heart. He tightened his hold as she seemed to cling to him. After a moment, he realized he was smelling strawberries. It must be a perfume or something she used.

He took some comfort that she wasn't crying about him. But it was clear her heart was breaking about something, and his instinct was to find out what was wrong and to fix it. He felt protective of her, and if this was about a boyfriend, he'd gladly confront the guy. Or maybe it was about one of her parents?

When she started to calm, he said, "Hey, my SUV is just down the road. We can get in and at least be warm. Do you want to go get coffee or something?"

She drew away from him and wiped at her face. "I don't want to go anywhere."

"We can just sit in the SUV, then?"

She hesitated, then nodded.

Jeff felt like he'd achieved a small victory. They walked down the street together, not touching, not speaking. When they reached his Land Rover, Jeff opened the passenger door for her. She climbed in, and he hurried around to the driver's side to start the engine. The radio came on, and he turned down the volume, leaving a little background noise. He thought it might help her relax.

"You can just drive," she said, her voice sounding a bit shaky.

Jeff was more than happy to oblige. He pulled onto the street and drove out of the neighborhood.

Alicia shoved her hands into her coat pockets and stared out her window. She wasn't looking at him, or talking to him, but at least she'd stopped crying. And she'd let him hold her. That had to count for something. Maybe she really had forgiven him for prom. Maybe, he thought with a flicker of new hope, maybe they could be friends again. It would never be the same, he knew, but with her living and working again in Pine Valley, they could at least put the past behind them.

Jeff didn't really have a goal in mind, but he drove toward the ski slopes. Most people were calling it a day, and the traffic going in the opposite direction was thick. But on the way up to the slopes, the lane was wide open. Jeff's phone had buzzed a couple of times with incoming texts, but he'd been ignoring them.

When it rang, Alicia said, "You can get that. I'm sure you're a busy man."

Jeff wasn't sure how to take her tone of voice, but when he glanced at the incoming call and saw that it was his receptionist, he picked up.

"Hi Clara," he said.

"Oh hey," she said. "You haven't answered my texts. The Jensens want to put in an offer."

Jeff exhaled. This was great news, but he didn't want to abandon Alicia right now. "Okay, can you start writing everything up, and I'll be in touch later. I've got some things to do right now."

Clara was a smart woman and clued in to the fact that Jeff couldn't talk much. "Are you sure? I've never really written up an offer."

"Just pull up one from another client and compare that," he said. "I'll look at it when I can." Clara agreed, and Jeff hung up with her.

He felt Alicia looking at him, so he glanced over.

"Why did you do that?"

"Do what?"

"Blow off work?" she asked.

He raised his brows. "Well, I was hoping we could be friends again. And, uh, friends help each other, right?"

She just stared at him for a moment with those hazel eyes of hers; then her mouth curved into the barest of smiles. But at least it was a smile, and he'd take what he could get at this point.

"I guess we *could* maybe be friends," she said. "I mean, I practically soaked your shirt with my tears."

"Exactly what I was thinking," Jeff said with a laugh. He had the sudden urge to grab her hand and squeeze it, but her hands were still stuffed in her pockets, and he probably shouldn't be grabbing her hand anyway.

He pulled into the parking lot of one of the ski slope areas. The lot was nearly empty, and only a few stragglers were loading up their skis and snowboards. Instead of parking by the lodge, Jeff kept driving toward one of the groomed trails.

"Isn't this for snowmobiling?" Alicia asked when they hit the trail.

"We can drive as far as the first meadow." Jeff pointed up ahead where a long wooden fence stood. "We'll have to stop by the fence though."

Alicia just nodded, so Jeff took that as a yes. He drove to where the fence separated the groomed trails from the deeper snow. He put the Land Rover in park but left the engine idling for now. He didn't want to presume too much. "Do you want a water bottle?"

"Sure," she said, tugging off her beanie and running her fingers through her hair.

Jeff handed one over to her from his stash behind the passenger's seat. Leaning close to her brought her scent of strawberries again. Maybe it was the shampoo she used, because strawberries were completely out of season.

He straightened and tried not to notice the way her eyes were still rimmed red and how it made him want to pull her into his arms again.

"Sometimes I come out here right before the sun sets," he said. "If we're lucky, we'll get to see a herd of deer come down and graze."

"What do they graze on?" Alicia asked, looking around.

"Winter grass grows on the other side of the fence," he said. "The fence shields it from the blowing snow, so the line of grass makes a nice little feeding trough."

"Hmm," Alicia said, a slight smile on her face. "How come I never knew about this?"

Jeff shrugged. "I guess I found out about it after you'd moved."

"You moved first."

Her tone was light, so Jeff took that as encouragement. "Maybe, but when I came back, you were gone."

Her brows lifted as their gazes connected. "Did you look for me?"

He didn't say anything for a moment, couldn't say anything. Then finally, he admitted, "Of course."

Seven

It was strange sitting with Jeff and talking like no time had passed, Alicia thought. So much time *had* passed. She'd forgotten how fun it was to tease him. She'd forgotten a lot of things, and just spending the past hour with him had brought a lot of it back. The way he bit his bottom lip when he considered a serious question. The way he watched her so closely. The way he seemed unbothered to take time out of his day to drive her around and just hang out. Memories of what he was like as a boy and teenager came flooding back.

That had all gotten mixed up somewhere around their junior year in high school when their bodies and hormones had made both of them topsy-turvy. Alicia could admit her part in things now, and looking back, she knew she was probably one moody girl during those years. Jeff had always been able to coax a laugh out of her, though, just like he had today.

When he told her about the first time he'd come to this cleared field and tried to feed some deer, yet was chased by a buck, Alicia couldn't help but laugh. He hadn't been wearing boots, so his dress shoes had sent him tumbling into the snow.

"I think the buck felt sorry for me when he saw how clumsy I was," Jeff said with a broad smile. His blue eyes seemed to soak her in, and she felt a flutter in her stomach that she promptly ignored. "He decided to turn away and leave me alone after that. No use kicking a man when he's down."

Alicia laughed, and she realized how good it felt to laugh. He hadn't asked her again why she'd been crying, besides the first mistaken assumption that it was over him, and for that she was grateful. Out here, in nature, and watching a vibrant orange sunset helped her put the issues with her mother in perspective. What if, she wondered, what if her mom was doing the best she could and even though her best seemed extremely weak, it was all that she was capable of?

"Look," Jeff said, interrupting her train of thought. "They're coming out now."

Sure enough, Alicia spotted some deer separating from the line of trees and emerging onto the meadow. Jeff turned off the engine of his SUV, and everything went absolutely quiet.

The deer were beautiful creatures, elegant as they traveled together, and Alicia counted fifteen of them. "It's like a whole herd," she whispered, thinking if she spoke any louder, the deer would somehow hear and be spooked. "Where's your buck?"

Jeff gave a quiet laugh. "I think he's long gone by now."

Alicia nodded and settled deeper into her coat. The air in the SUV had started to cool already. She felt comfortable with Jeff, as if it hadn't been ten years since they'd talked. "My mother has become a hoarder," she said in a quiet voice as she watched the deer bend their heads to eat.

Jeff looked over at her. "A hoarder? As in, she collects stuff?"

"More than that," Alicia said, meeting his gaze. "She won't throw anything away. She orders stuff online all of the time with her alimony from my dad and the disability she's gotten from the state when she lost her job last year. She doesn't leave the house anymore. We got into a fight about this today because I threw away thirty-year-old hot pads."

Jeff blinked. "They must have been really important to her."

Alicia hadn't expected this response. She'd expected him to be shocked about the deterioration of her mom. "They were a wedding present. But in my defense, they were so ruined I couldn't even wash them."

Jeff leaned his head back and exhaled. "Is your mom why you came back to Pine Valley?"

Alicia nodded, feeling the tears burn her eyes again. She wouldn't let herself cry a second time on Jeff's shoulder. She drew in a shaky breath, then told him everything. The good, the bad, the ugly. How her mother was nearly arrested. How her father wanted Alicia to move on with her life and leave her mom's care to the state system—which would probably end up in jail time because of her habit of sorting through the neighborhood trash. How she didn't love having to work as a restaurant hostess and waste her college degree in business marketing.

At that confession, Jeff stopped her. "You have a marketing degree?"

"Yep," she said. "I thought about looking about town for a job, but working in the evenings is actually better than dealing with my mom. She takes late naps, and so she's asleep most of the time I'm gone, which means she can get into less trouble."

"You mean she can collect less of the neighbors' garbage?"

"Yeah," Alicia said. "The whole neighborhood knows about it, and it's like everyone is watching for her. I swear I feel them staring out their windows at me when I'm outside."

"That must be rough," Jeff said. "I had no idea your mom was having such a hard time."

Alicia shrugged. "No one does, not even Gwen." When she saw the questioning look on Jeff's face, she added. "Gwen's my friend at the restaurant."

"Ah, that's right," he said. "I saw a picture of the both of you on Facebook."

"What?"

Jeff's face reddened, and Alicia decided not to find that adorable.

"I, uh, I sent you a friend request after I saw you last night," he continued. "I wanted to find a way to apologize."

Alicia pulled out her phone. She hadn't been on Facebook today, and she opened the app. "There's your request." She looked over at him, and he gave her a hopeful smile. Alicia laughed, then clicked "confirm."

"It's official," Jeff said. "We're friends."

She smiled. "It's official."

Jeff laughed, and Alicia wanted to capture that laugh and let it wash over her when she'd need it the most.

His phone rang, and he glanced at it.

"You can get it," she said. "I mean, I've kept you long enough from work." She hadn't meant to look at the screen on his phone, but when she saw the name Paige, Alicia had the impression it wasn't a work call.

"Uh, it's not work," Jeff said, staring at the phone like he was in a trance.

"Oh, your girlfriend." Alicia waved at the phone. "Seriously, you can answer it. I won't make a peep."

But the phone had stopped ringing.

"Do you want to call her back?"

Jeff finally met her gaze. "Paige and I have been dating, but it's not all that serious," he said, his tone sounding uncomfortable.

His phone started ringing again, and Alicia couldn't help but look at the screen. *Paige,* again.

"Hang on," Jeff said, opening his door and jumping out. He shut the door, then answered his phone.

Alicia might have felt offended that he didn't want her to overhear his conversation, but it wasn't really any of her business. She and Jeff were just becoming reacquainted, and while she'd told him some personal things about her mom, they really didn't know each other. So what did she expect? It was nearly dark, and the deer were moving back into the trees to find their warm copse for the night.

She watched Jeff pace in the packed snow, his breath looking like white smoke. He didn't look happy. Paige seemed to be a high-maintenance woman, and Alicia wondered what Jeff saw in her besides her obviously perfect looks. Alicia knew she shouldn't judge. It wasn't like her own life was all that great. And maybe Paige was an amazing person beneath her immaculate veneer.

But watching Jeff pace, and the tense set of his broad shoulders, made her wonder if things weren't how they seemed between Jeff and Paige. Even beautiful people had problems, she decided.

Jeff walked back toward the SUV, apparently off his phone call with Paige. He opened the door and climbed in, then started the ignition. When he didn't put the SUV into drive, Alicia said, "Is everything all right?"

He didn't say anything for a minute. Then he looked over at her, and Alicia could clearly see the stress on his face. "Not really," he said at last. "We broke up."

Alicia blinked. "Just now?"

He gave a slow nod. "At least, I think so." He leaned his head against the seat and closed his eyes.

Alicia looked away from his handsome, but tortured profile. Had he been in love with Paige? Had she dumped him, or was it the other way around? Or were they one of those on-again, off-again couples?

"I'm sorry," she said, because no matter which way the break-up happened, it would still be an emotional drain.

"Me too." He opened his eyes and put the SUV into drive. He drove across the clearing, then along the groomed trail. When they reached the parking lot, it was empty, and he picked up speed as they pulled onto the canyon road.

Alicia didn't dare press for more details about Paige or the break-up; it wasn't like they were best friends anymore. She wondered what would happen after he dropped her off at her house. Would he ask for her number? Would they keep in touch? Or would their friendship be reduced to liking each other's pictures on social media?

The thought made her feel numb. The past couple of hours with Jeff had been cathartic. And it was all about to end. He was obviously going through some drama, and she had no right to put her burdens on him.

Although the heater of the SUV quickly warmed up the interior, Alicia stayed burrowed in her coat, keeping herself isolated from a rush of past feelings. Feelings of protectiveness of Jeff, feelings of wanting to spend more time with him, feelings of what it was like to have a best friend. She had to forget all of that, and the sooner, the better.

Eight

Jeff watched Alicia walk into her mom's house. When she shut the front door, he backed out of the driveway. The house looked like it could use some outside repairs, and from Alicia's explanations about her mom, he assumed the inside probably could as well. Jeff wasn't much of a handyman, but he could call up his friend Grant, who was an expert craftsman and ran a construction business with his brother-in-law. Jeff had hired Grant to do fix ups before, and he could ask him to give the Waters a good deal, or Jeff could even pay for it himself. Alicia's mom was on a fixed income, and Alicia probably wasn't raking in the money working at the restaurant.

Helping out Alicia was the least he could do. A sort of apology, he supposed, even though Alicia had told him he didn't owe her anything. He knew she'd refuse if he offered, so he'd just set it up. Except now he was hesitating. The drive back from the ski resort had been quiet, and that had been Jeff's fault. His mood had plummeted after being railed on by

Paige. And he couldn't come up with something inane to talk about with Alicia.

When he'd told Paige he wanted to meet somewhere and talk, she'd immediately set in on him, asking him point blank if he was breaking up with her. No matter how many times he said he'd rather talk in person, she dragged his confession out of him. And when he did admit, over the phone, that he wanted to call things off, she'd gone ballistic.

The names she called him hadn't been deserved. Their recent dates had been more and more tense, filled with complaints from Paige about how little time they spent together and how busy Jeff was. The more time he spent with Paige, the more he realized they had little in common. When he told her that he didn't want to be with someone who didn't trust him and constantly questioned him about ex-girlfriends, Paige had told him that he'd always be a playboy. She asked him when he'd ever dated someone more than a few months.

He couldn't answer that, because he'd never dated anyone more than a few months.

As he pulled up to his office, he saw that Clara was already gone. A couple more texts had come in from her with questions about the Jensens' offer, but he hadn't replied yet. He parked and unlocked the back door. The stray cat was nowhere to be seen—it was probably out enjoying the night life, or whatever cats did with their night vision.

As he turned on the lights, then the laptop, he wondered if Paige was right. Was he a playboy? His longest friendship with a girl/woman had been with Alicia, but he'd blown that in high school. As he pulled up the Jensens' offer, he wondered if maybe he hadn't allowed himself to be serious with a woman *because* of Alicia.

He sat back in his chair and sighed. That was ridiculous.

Until last night, he hadn't seen or spoken to her for ten years. He just hadn't found someone he could see himself spending the rest of his life with. It wasn't that he was a playboy, he was just . . . still looking.

Focus. His brain was starting to feel numb, and he wanted to get this offer submitted before he crashed. He read through what Clara had put together, adjusted a handful of things, then emailed it to the seller. Then he texted Clara to let her know that it was submitted and there was a forty-eight-hour contingent on the offer.

Done.

Jeff yawned and stretched. He should really go through the rest of his emails and return some texts. But most people had called it a day—most normal people who had families or social lives. He propped his chin on his hands and closed his eyes for a moment. He was grateful that Alicia had stopped to talk to him, that she'd shared her troubles, and that they'd begun a friendship. At least, he hoped they had. Was this afternoon a one-time thing?

When he'd dropped her off, they hadn't made any plans to meet again. They hadn't exchanged numbers. Jeff should have asked for her number, but would that have been too forward or presumptuous?

Had Paige's accusations been right? Was he only a playboy when it came to women? Or could he be a good friend? He hoped he could be a friend to Alicia. In the morning, he'd call Grant and see what he could arrange to get some work done on the Waters house. Or maybe he should reach out to Grant tonight.

That was his last thought before Jeff realized he'd fallen asleep with his head resting on his arms atop his desk. He lifted his head and looked around. He felt disoriented, and he looked at the decorative clock on the wall. It was 1:00 a.m. The lights were still on, but the laptop had powered off. And something was rustling in the back room.

Jeff froze, listening. Had someone broken in? Surely a robber wouldn't break in when the office lights were on. He rose to his feet, his body and neck stiff from sleeping at a desk. Then he heard a meow.

The cat. It walked out of the back room and meowed again.

"How did you get in here?" Jeff said, peering down at the scraggly calico. He walked toward it, but it turned and trotted to the back door. Jeff followed and opened the door, and the cat darted out. Probably to use the bathroom.

He walked into the back room and flipped on the light. The corner where Clara kept the cat food looked like the cat had helped himself. And apparently the cat had slept on a padded folding chair, if the stray hair was any indication.

Jeff shook his head. How had he come to this? Falling asleep in his office? Chasing down Alicia. Breaking up with Paige. Running on empty?

He turned off the office lights and exited the building, locking up the place. Then he jumped into his cold SUV and made the drive back home. He probably wouldn't be able to get any real sleep, but at least he could get cleaned up and not scare away his clients.

After his shower, he found enough fixings to make a double-decker sandwich, and he sat at the granite island of his kitchen. His home had undergone extensive renovations before he'd moved into it. He appreciated the space compared to his former condo, but right now it felt cavernous and empty. Lonely somehow, like him.

He didn't understand his emotions. He'd wanted to break things off with Paige, so it wasn't as if he was missing her. Far from it. He was relieved. He felt like he was missing someone though, and the couple of hours with Alicia had made him feel less alone.

Jeff blew out a breath. He had to stop letting his thoughts circle. He had too much to do without letting himself get side-tracked.

He picked up his phone, thinking about sending Alicia a message to tell her about Grant and some of the work he could do on the outside of her house. He didn't know if she'd be appreciative or defensive. But he didn't have her cell number, so his only choice was to message her through Facebook.

It was 2:00 a.m. now, and if she noticed the time stamp, she might think he was creepy. Or a work-a-holic, which he readily admitted, and Paige hated about him. But he sent a message anyway: *Hey, I hope work went well tonight. I forgot to get your cell number, so, you know, we could be friends.*

Simple. Casual. Light-hearted.

He'd just finished off his sandwich when his phone dinged. He picked it up; Alicia had messaged him back.

Do you have insomnia or something? Here's my number . . . What's yours?

Jeff grinned. He opened his contacts and put in her number. Then he sent her a text: *This is Jeff. And I fell asleep at the office last night. So here I am. Wide awake.*

Her reply: *Jeff who?*

He laughed. *Funny. Do you have insomnia?*

She didn't reply back right away, so he cleaned up the kitchen while he waited. When his phone rang, he was shocked to see her name pop up on the screen. He took a breath before answering. "Hey."

"Hey."

He leaned against the counter, trying to summon up every bit of casualness he could to counteract the racing of his pulse. It was just Alicia. The girl he'd grown up with. "Can't sleep? Or are you usually up this early?" He didn't want to tell her he knew about her early morning trips to the dumpster.

"Can't sleep," she said.

Her voice sounded a little scratchy to Jeff. Sexy, actually. But he focused on the *scratchy* description. "How was the restaurant?"

"Busy," she said. "But not as busy as Valentine's was. Gwen wasn't on shift, so it seemed like the hours crawled by."

"I wouldn't know," Jeff said, moving from the kitchen to the living room, where he settled on the couch. "I was having a nice nap at my desk."

Her laughter was soft. "How's your neck?"

"Painful." He leaned back on the couch. "I should probably take Advil or something."

"I don't think I've ever fallen asleep at a desk."

"Not even in college?"

"Nope," she said, amusement in her voice. "I'm talented enough to make it to my bed."

Jeff smiled. "How do you know it doesn't take talent to fall asleep at a desk? I mean, you have to be able to sleep and not fall off your chair."

"That's true."

He could hear the smile in her voice.

"But the real question is, can you sleep on planes?" she asked.

"I can, and I have," Jeff proclaimed.

"Then you definitely win," Alicia said.

"What do I win?" he asked.

"The prize for being a talented sleeper."

Jeff laughed. He had forgotten how much he loved talking to Alicia. He'd missed her. He'd missed this. "Are you working tomorrow, I mean, today?"

"Yeah, I work every night," she said. "It's my break from my mom, so I don't mind. Ironic, huh?"

"So not much of a night life, I guess," Jeff said.

"No, I live vicariously through everyone who comes to the restaurant," Alicia said with a self-deprecating laugh. "Sometimes I hang out with Gwen when our schedules work out. I'm sort of a pathetic friend, so you might want to rethink us."

"I don't believe you for a moment," Jeff said. "You're pretty amazing, Alicia."

Nine

Was Jeff flirting with her? Alicia brushed off his "amazing" compliment. She wasn't fishing for compliments anyway. When he'd messaged her his number on Facebook, she didn't know why she decided to call him. It just seemed so juvenile to trade messages when they could talk on the phone. Now that they were talking, Alicia had curled beneath the pile of blankets on her bed—there were never any shortages of blankets in her house, thanks to her mom.

Whether or not Jeff was flirting, or just being nice, she loved listening to the low tones of his voice coming through the phone. His adult voice was familiar, yet different too—deeper, richer, masculine.

"You've always been generous with the compliments," Alicia told him, trying to deflect the uncomfortableness that grew inside when people complimented her.

"Telling you that you're amazing isn't a compliment," he said. "It's the plain truth. Don't tell me you still can't take a compliment after all these years?"

"Well, I don't have a problem with compliments in general, especially when they're earned."

"Look," Jeff said. "Not that I want to argue with you, but you just left your entire life behind to come home and take care of your mom. If that's not amazing, then I don't know what is."

His tone was teasing, but Alicia didn't want to be complimented on this part of her life. She should have probably let it drop, told him thank you, and asked him about his work or something. Instead she said, "It's not amazing when I'm probably making it worse. Yeah, I'm keeping her out of jail—at least, I think I am—it's not like I'm here twenty-four-seven. But I've caused her plenty of grief and interfered with her routine. Just because I'm here doesn't mean I'm the most loving and compassionate daughter. I know it causes her even more anxiety to have someone in the house, touching her stuff, moving things around, and she's always paranoid I'm going to throw something away . . . which I've done plenty of times, although I'm pretty good at hiding it."

But Jeff wasn't buying it. "Of course it's hard, and of course you have some resentment. The amazing part I'm talking about is that you are there, you are trying, and you haven't given up."

"Yet." Alicia didn't know why she was being so negative, but something about Jeff made her feel safe to be vulnerable—at least about this.

He gave a half-laugh. "Yet? Even if you left tomorrow, you've been helping her for months. That's pretty incredible in my book, sweetheart."

She knew he wasn't calling her sweetheart in any romantic way, but the endearment filled her with warmth. She thought about what she'd done for her mother over the past few months. It hadn't been perfect, but Alicia had been there.

"Thank you, Jeff," she finally said. It felt good to have someone acknowledge her sacrifice and her love for her mom. Jeff's words had made her feel stronger and like she wasn't so alone in all of this.

"So, how are *you* doing?" she asked, pulling a pillow against her chest. "I mean, you just broke up with your girl-friend, and here I am, unloading my problems onto you."

"I'm fine," he said. "It's just been a crazy week, and the thing with Paige is just another situation to add to the mess."

"The mess?" Alicia asked. Was *she* a part of that mess?

"I've got court in a few hours where a judge will determine whether or not my former business partner has to pay back the $400,000 he embezzled from our company, or if it's money that was owed to him." Jeff exhaled. "Long story, but I'm hoping that after court I can finally get back to normal."

"Wow," she said. "I'm really sorry. Was your partner doing real estate with you?"

"Yeah," Jeff said. "Remember my cousin Kyle?"

She had a vague recollection of a blond kid who used to stare at her a lot when he came to visit the Finch family. "I do."

"He was my partner," he said, some bitterness in his voice. "Didn't think I could go wrong with family. We both put in some of our own money to start up our own real estate company a few years ago when Pine Valley was starting to explode. I also got a business loan under my name so we could cover office rent and other business expenses while waiting for commissions to come in. Kyle had the degree in business finance, so he was co-owner and CFO. I'm the people person, so I worked with most of the clients. Kyle was on vacation with his wife when I met a new client for lunch. I used the business credit card, and when it was declined, I didn't think much of it. Later I texted Kyle to tell him that the balance must be low since the card was declined. I asked him to transfer some money from our business loan into the business checking account if needed. We had a couple of big commissions coming in, but they hadn't funded yet."

"And that's when you found out?" Alicia said.

"That was just the beginning," Jeff said. "Without Kyle around to get the mail, I received a bunch of junk mail from business loan sharks. I knew enough that those types of letters don't come unless your accounts are maxed out. Banks say they don't share financial information, but it's shared nonetheless. When Kyle came back, I demanded to see the accounting. He'd pulled out two more loans under my name and credit. We were $300,000 in debt, and none of that money had gone to our business expenses. Those had been well covered by commissions. We got into a pretty heated argument, and I told him we needed to hire an outside company to handle all the accounting. Kyle agreed, or I thought he had. A week later, he moved his family out of Pine Valley, and the two commissions that came in had been withdrawn. Nearly $100,000 gone like that."

"Wow, I can't even imagine," Alicia said. "First, it's your cousin, second, it's a ton of money. How long ago was it?"

"It's been dragging on for a year," Jeff said. "Thankfully, my lawyer had been able to stop all the creditors from destroying my finances. They are on hold until the case is settled. I'm making decent money on my own, and all the clientele I built up early on has been paying off very well the last two years. But $400,000 is still a huge chunk to be responsible for."

Alicia nodded, even though Jeff couldn't see her. "The judge won't try to make you pay for it, will he?"

"My lawyer is pretty confident we'll win, and I'll be

absolved of all debt and responsibility," he said. "But until I hear the verdict for myself, I can't help having my doubts."

"I don't blame you," Alicia said. "I can't imagine a judge not ruling in your favor. No wonder you can't sleep."

They were both silent. "I feel bad for Kyle's wife," she said after a moment.

"Yeah," Jeff said. "She actually divorced him. It's probably finalized by now. I say good riddance."

"I guess no one's life is what we think it is," Alicia said. "Looking at your social media, one would think you have it made."

"You've been looking at my social media?"

Alicia's face heated. "I mean . . . I'm *assuming* your social media shows the good life. Everyone can see that you have nice cars, and you're a good-looking, successful man." Okay, she needed to stop talking.

"Hmm, I don't know if I've ever heard so many compliments from you in one sentence," Jeff teased.

She groaned. "Don't let it go to your huge head." She was really glad he couldn't see her blushing.

"My huge, *good-looking* head?" he said.

"Ha. Ha." She shifted her position in bed. "I think you'd better sleep before you have to go to court."

"Yeah, you're probably right," he said in a quieter, more sober tone. "Thanks for calling. It was great to vent, and to laugh. I needed that."

"Me too," Alicia said. She was reluctant to hang up, but it was nearly 3:00 in the morning. Her mom was always more agitated in the mornings, so Alicia didn't want to be dead tired. She decided to skip the 4:30 garbage run. "Good luck at court."

"Thanks," he said. "I'll need it."

Alicia hesitated, then said, "Let me know how it goes."

He seemed to hesitate too. "I will."

When they hung up, Alicia stared at her phone for a moment. It had been a bold move calling him in the middle of the night. But Jeff was right; it had been really nice to vent and laugh. She couldn't imagine facing a court appearance and having to rely on a judge to determine her future. She hadn't asked him what time he was going to court. So she wouldn't know whether or not he was late in calling her. Not that he owed her anything.

Alicia plugged in her phone and burrowed under her covers. She hoped Jeff would get some real sleep. He deserved it.

Ten

"Hey, baby," the voicemail from Paige said. "I just remembered you have court today. I didn't want you to go in there without hearing from me first. I'm really sorry about our fight, and I want to make it up to you. Call me right after, and we can go eat somewhere. I've been starving all day. Bye, babe."

Jeff deleted the voicemail before he climbed out of his Lamborghini. He'd only driven the thing because he wanted Kyle to see it. Maybe it was chest-pounding at its worst, but Jeff didn't care. He'd fallen asleep for a couple of hours this morning after talking to Alicia, but he woke up feeling edgy. He guessed court dates did that to a person. And ex-girlfriends calling to make up.

"I was about to call you," someone spoke behind him. "You're late."

Jeff turned to see his lawyer, Dawson Harris. He was dressed in one of his fancy suits, and his wavy brown hair reminded Jeff of a Ken doll. Dawson was only a couple of years older than Jeff but had already made a name for himself in winning several big cases that were written up in the local paper. Dawson's main office was in the next city over, but he was also a fixture in Pine Valley. He even had a condo at the ski resort.

"I'm only five minutes late," Jeff said, shaking Dawson's hand, then letting go.

"That's late in my book." Dawson raised his brows. "You're wound pretty tight. I told you, the case is solid, and the judge will rule in your favor."

"I hope so," Jeff said. "Or I'm driving this thing back to the dealership."

Dawson shook his head. "If I was a betting man, I'd bet that you'll be taking your girlfriend out tonight in this car."

"You just lost the bet. I'm a single man now," Jeff said.

"What? I thought you were dating a lady named Paige."

"Long story." Jeff locked the car and walked with Dawson across the parking lot. "Maybe if we have something to celebrate after court, I'll buy dinner and tell you the gory details."

Dawson barked out a laugh. "You can buy me dinner, but I don't want to know the details. I have enough break-up stories of my own to try to forget."

"I thought you were married," Jeff said, glancing over at him as they reached the glass doors of the courthouse.

"*Was* married." Dawson pulled open the door and waved Jeff to go inside first. "Let's just say you're not the only one who's had a crappy year."

It wasn't really the time or place to quiz Dawson more. Besides, after today, and possibly dinner tonight, Jeff hoped he wouldn't have to see Dawson again . . . at least for legal reasons.

Jeff stepped up to the security station they had to go

through before entering the court building. He put his phone, keys, and wallet into a plastic bin. Then he slid off his shoes and put them in a plastic bin as well.

"Your ID, please," the female security guard with a severe bun said.

"Oh, sorry." Jeff fished his driver's license out of his wallet and handed it over to the woman. She took quite a while to compare the picture to Jeff's likeness.

"I can vouch for him," Dawson said.

The security guard threw Dawson a glare. "Let me do my job, Mr. Harris, and yours will be much more pleasant."

"Just trying to help," Dawson said, lifting his hands as if he was surrendering.

The security guard scoffed, but a small smile escaped.

"You might want to frisk those guys," Dawson said, nodding his head toward a group of people who had just arrived at the doors.

Jeff glanced over. Kyle was walking in with his lawyers. Did he really need two of them? Behind the lawyers walked Uncle Rick.

Jeff wanted to groan. Why did Kyle have to bring his dad? This had all been hard enough on the family already. Their dads were brothers, and Jeff had told his own parents to steer clear of the court proceedings. Kyle looked like he'd lost weight, and his blond hairline appeared to have receded. Uncle Rick was an older version of Kyle—a little more heavily set and nearly bald.

Jeff moved through the security scanner and, without looking back, put on his shoes and gathered up his things.

"Meet me in conference room number two," Dawson told him.

Jeff was only too happy to abandon the front lobby and not be faced with any sort of conversation with Kyle or Uncle

Rick. Nothing good could come of a conversation before the judge handed down his decision.

Waiting in the small conference room by himself, Jeff scrolled through his phone if only to ignore his nerves. He went to his call log and deleted the evidence of Paige's phone call. He pulled up the call log from the conversation with Alicia. They'd talked for almost an hour. As he was remembering some of their conversation, a text came through . . . from Alicia.

Crossing fingers for you! Hope it goes well and the judge is a smart man. Or woman.

Jeff smiled to himself. He should probably not respond because Dawson would show up any second. *The judge is a man, and Dawson says he's a fair judge. I'm definitely crossing my fingers as well. But I'm still nervous.*

Her reply came seconds later. *You've done everything right. Hopefully your lawyer will earn his money.*

Jeff was still smiling when Dawson entered the room. "Something funny?"

He pocketed his phone. "Just texting a friend."

Dawson raised his brows but didn't ask more questions. "Kyle's attorney says they'll countersue if they lose the case."

Jeff exhaled. "Can they do that?"

"Of course, but we'll see how much money your cousin wants to keep spending, especially if his wages are garnished."

"I just want it to be over with," Jeff said.

"The bright side will be that we can keep hanging out together." Dawson cracked a smile.

"Lucky me," Jeff said in a dry tone.

"Ready to get this moving?" Dawson said. "The judge should be leaving his chambers in a few minutes, and we need to be seated before he arrives. If there's anyone more punctual than me, it's Judge Christensen."

Jeff rose to his feet. "I'm ready." He walked with Dawson out of the conference room and into the court room.

Forty minutes later, Jeff and Dawson strode out of the courtroom ahead of Kyle and his council. They didn't say a word until they reached Jeff's Lamborghini.

"I guess I'm buying dinner after all," Jeff said, turning to Dawson with a grin.

"Yep, I guess you are."

Jeff stuck out his hand to shake Dawson's, then pulled him into a bear hug.

Dawson laughed and slapped Jeff's back. "If Kyle makes good on his threat to countersue, this isn't quite over yet."

"I know," Jeff said, stepping away from Dawson. "But let's celebrate this victory."

Dawson grinned. "Sounds good to me. Where are we going?"

"I'll meet you at the Alpine Lodge at 7:30," Jeff said.

Dawson's eyebrows shot up. "You have reservations?"

"Not exactly," Jeff said. "But I have connections."

Dawson shook his head with a grin. "Of course you do. See you at 7:30 p.m., and congratulations."

"Thanks for everything," Jeff said. When Dawson had walked to his car, Jeff slid into his and roared out of the parking lot just as Kyle exited the building. Jeff didn't need to look over at his cousin to know that the man was pretty much hating him now.

Payback was bitter, that was sure.

As Jeff headed to his house to change before going into the office, he finally started to relax, and exhaustion took over. If he didn't have to catch up on work, he knew he could easily fall asleep. Instead, he went home, changed into khakis and a button-down shirt, then climbed into his car again. He didn't check his phone for texts or emails. For a few minutes, he just wanted to enjoy the moment of victory.

The judge had ruled in Jeff's favor, and Kyle's wages would be garnished until the debts were paid back. Jeff's name was cleared of all responsibility toward the creditors, and his record would be wiped clean by the court. Jeff knew Kyle was going to file for bankruptcy, and there was a good chance he'd countersue. But the lawyer who agreed to represent a bankrupt Kyle would be a fool.

As Jeff headed out of his neighborhood in his SUV, he slowed when he turned the corner and spotted a small florist shop. He had the sudden urge to buy flowers and give them to someone who'd helped him get through the last day. He stopped at the curb in front of the shop and hurried inside. He bought a mixed flower bouquet, then found himself driving to his old neighborhood. There, everything seemed quiet in the late afternoon. He didn't know what time Alicia's shift was tonight, but he hoped she'd be home. All indicators were that she was home, since her car was in the driveway.

When he rang the doorbell, he heard footsteps coming from inside. Then there was silence. Alicia or her mother was probably looking through the peephole. Eventually, the door opened a cracked.

"What do you want?" a woman's voice asked.

It wasn't Alicia's voice, so it must be her mom's. "Mrs. Waters? It's Jeff Finch."

The door opened another half-inch. With the darkness of the interior behind her, Jeff couldn't really get a good look at Mrs. Waters. And she seemed extremely reluctant to speak to him.

"How are you doing?" he asked when she said nothing.

"What do you want?"

The question was harsh, but Jeff didn't let it deter him. Alicia had told him about her mom's difficulties, and all he could think of was how he probably didn't understand how much she'd truly changed. "I'm looking for Alicia. Is she home?"

The woman scoffed, or something close to it. "She's always gone. Gone to work. Gone shopping. Gone who knows where. I'm not her secretary." Then, she shut the door.

Jeff stared, unblinking, not sure of what just happened. "Mrs. Waters?" he called out, knowing that she could hear him through the door. "I've brought some flowers over. Do you want me to leave them on the porch?"

He waited a moment, then longer. Finally, he was about to set the flowers on the porch when the door cracked open again. Jeff straightened. Mrs. Finch stood there in a blue bathrobe that looked like it had been run over multiple times by a truck. She was folding her thin arms, and her glaring gaze was zeroed in on him. The gauntness of her face and the dark circles beneath her eyes made Jeff think of a prisoner of war victim. In a word, she looked terrible. Not the Mrs. Waters he remembered at all.

"I used to live next door," Jeff said, scrambling for something to say that might help her recognize him. They'd all changed over the years.

"I know who you are," Mrs. Waters said, her tone still hostile. "What are you doing here?"

Jeff held up the flowers. "I've brought flowers for Alicia."

"I already know that." She leaned against the door, keeping it open to only reveal her thin frame, and nothing else behind. "But why are you here? Why are you bothering Alicia? You've done enough harm to our family."

Jeff was speechless. Harm to their *family*? His stomach felt like he'd swallowed a rock. "I—I'm sorry. I didn't mean to—"

"Just leave those on the porch," Mrs. Waters said. "If Alicia wants them, she can bring them in herself." She shut the door again, and this time Jeff heard the lock slide into place.

He stood on the porch for several moments, truly not knowing what to do. Should he call Alicia? Should he just leave the flowers? Should he take the flowers with him? Finally, he set the flowers on the porch and walked back to his SUV. Would Mrs. Waters tell her daughter that he was there? What had Alicia told her mom about him?

Jeff's good mood had completely deflated. Especially since it seemed that Mrs. Waters blamed him for much more than being an idiot in high school. Did she really blame him for harming their whole family?

When he was pulling up to his office, his phone rang. *Alicia.* He hesitated for a second, debating whether to answer it. He was feeling pretty defensive, and that probably wasn't a good way to feel before answering the phone.

Finally he answered, "Hello."

"Jeff?" Alicia said. "My mom said you came by with flowers. I can't believe she made you leave them on the front porch. I'm so sorry."

"I don't think she wanted me to leave them in the first place."

She groaned. "What did my mom say to you?"

The distress in her voice was thawing Jeff's defensiveness. "Uh, she just wasn't happy to see me, that's all. I probably shouldn't have dropped in like that."

"No, I mean, yes, it's all right that you dropped in," she said. "We don't usually get visitors . . . I guess you can see why."

"I don't know if having visitors was really your mom's concern," he said. "I obviously need to apologize to her, too."

Alicia was quiet for a moment, and when she spoke next, her voice was trembling. "Please tell me what she said. I need to know. She can't get away with being cruel to my friends."

The fact that Alicia was still considering him a "friend" was heartening. But he wondered how much truth was in what Mrs. Waters had accused him of. He told Alicia the entire conversation, not leaving out one word or detail. When he finished, he thought he heard her sniffle. "I didn't mean to upset you or make it worse."

"I'm so sorry about her," Alicia said, and Jeff knew she was crying.

He felt awful. "Don't apologize for your mom. It's not *you*, Alicia. She's responsible for her own actions. But what she said to me made me realize that your mom was hurt over my actions too."

Alicia sniffled. "She was, but that's no excuse. It's partly my fault because I didn't tell her we were hanging out. I don't want you to take what she said personally. That's how she treats everyone, and that's something we're working on with her therapist."

"What can I do to apologize to your mom?" Jeff said.

"You don't owe her anything." Alicia's voice was stronger now.

"I want to make things right," he said. "I mean, if we're going to be friends, then I'll probably run into your mom once in a while, and I don't want her to be angry at me."

Alicia sighed. "She's always angry." Her voice softened. "The flowers are beautiful."

"I'm glad you like them," he said, his spirits starting to lift.

"Why did you get *me* flowers, and how did your court date go?" she asked.

"I got you flowers because I'm glad we're friends again," Jeff said with a laugh. "And the judge ruled in my favor."

"Wow, I'm so happy for you," Alicia said. "I knew it! But I'm still so glad it actually happened."

"Me too," he said. "Kyle has threatened to counter-sue, but my lawyer isn't too worried the case will hold water. He thinks Kyle is going to file for bankruptcy, and if that's the case, he'll have a hard time retaining a lawyer to represent his lawsuit."

"Kyle's crazy," Alicia said.

"You're telling me."

"I guess you have to celebrate today's victory, right?" she said. "I'll bet your parents are thrilled."

"I haven't talked to them yet," Jeff said. "I grabbed the flowers for you, and I just got to the office. My secretary is probably sick of me being AWOL."

"I'm flattered to be the one getting flowers on your big day," Alicia said. "What are you doing for yourself?"

"Uh, I'm taking my lawyer out for dinner tonight, does that count?" Jeff said.

"Depends on the place."

It was good to hear laughter in her voice.

"Actually, I was hoping we could get a table at your restaurant," Jeff said. "Say around 7:30?"

"I see how it is," she said. "The flowers were a bribe."

He grinned. "Maybe just a little."

Alicia laughed. "All right, *friend.* I'll see what I can do."

When they hung up, Jeff turned off the engine of the SUV and climbed out. He walked into his office to find Clara sitting at her desk, on the phone. Clara was a vivacious redhead a couple of years younger than Jeff. She was outgoing and friendly, and although Jeff worked well with her, Clara could also wear him out. Two extroverts wore each other out after a while. She waved at him, and he nodded. Then he settled at his own desk and pulled up his emails.

When Clara got off the phone she came in and sat down. "Well, look at you. I thought I'd have to put out a manhunt for you."

Jeff turned to look over at a grinning Clara.

"Court's over, and now I can focus on moving forward."

Clara raised her brows. "Sounds like court went great?"

"Judge ruled in my favor—"

Clara let out a whoop, and Jeff laughed.

"You're happy," she said.

It was his turn to raise his eyebrows. "I'm relieved. I didn't know what a weight it had been until today."

Clara nodded, still watching him closely. "It's something else. More than just the court thing. Are you and Paige getting serious? Is there an engagement on the horizon?"

"No, nothing like that," Jeff said. "In fact, we broke up last night." At least, he'd tried to break up. He'd forgotten about her message until now. It seemed he needed to have another conversation with her.

"Oh, I'm so sorry," Clara said, her forehead wrinkling. She rose to her feet, and Jeff thought she might come over and hug him. Clara was like that.

He waved her off. "I'm fine, actually. I'm better than fine."

Clara tilted her head, and folded her arms. "Well, I can see that. What's going on, boss?"

His phone rang, and the timing couldn't be better. "I should take this."

Clara pursed her lips, but her eyes were still bright and filled with amusement as she sat back down at her desk.

Eleven

$\mathcal{A}$licia found her mom sitting cross-legged on the floor, flipping through a catalog that was at least ten years old. She had the gas fireplace turned up all the way, and the front room was way too warm for Alicia's taste, but she didn't want to deal with that right now. What she needed to deal with was how her mom had treated Jeff when he brought the flowers.

"Hi, Mom," Alicia said, sitting down on the rickety rocking chair that had been a fixture in their home for as long as she could remember.

Her mom didn't answer or look up.

"I talked to Jeff on the phone," Alicia said, deciding to get right to the point.

Her mom's gaze snapped up. "I hope you gave him a piece of your mind."

Alicia sighed. "Look, Mom, I should have told you this earlier, but Jeff and I have started to be friends again."

"Since when?" Her mom narrowed her eyes.

"Since just a couple of days ago," Alicia said. "He . . . came into the restaurant, and well, he apologized for what happened our senior year."

"I'm sure he did—he probably didn't want to lose his reservation."

Her mom wasn't going to make this easy, and Alicia didn't want to give her any more details than necessary. If the past few months were any indicator, her mom would use any little thing against Jeff. "His apology was genuine," Alicia said. It was strange to be in a position of defending Jeff. For so many years, she'd also held a grudge. "He's really trying, and he even wants to apologize to you."

With a scoff, her mom pulled her knees up and hugged them against her chest. "It's a little too late for that. Look at you. You're being gullible. Didn't you learn your lesson last time?"

Mom, that was ten years ago," Alicia said, annoyed that she had to rehash all of this. "We were dumb teenagers. My crush is long over, and he . . . well, he's a grown man who is a decent person. We're friends, that's it. No expectations."

"Ha." Her mom scratched at her unwashed hair. "Friends? You know a single man and a single woman who are attracted to each other can't ever really be friends."

Alicia threw up her hands. "I'm not attracted to him! And he's not attracted to me!" She didn't mean to yell, but it was either that or cry.

Her mom pulled her robe tighter about her body as if she could possibly be cold in this stifling room. "So, he just brought you flowers because he had nothing better to do? And don't play me stupid, girl, I saw what he looked like. Fancy clothes. Expensive car. Probably spends every weekend at the spa."

"Mom! That's not fair," Alicia said. "We can't judge him that way. He brought me flowers because he was . . ."

"He was what?"

Alicia sighed. "Because he just finished a hard day, and well, last night we talked for a while. And the flowers were like a thank you for our talk, I guess."

Her mom rose to her feet and walked to the fireplace. Holding out her hands to the fake flames, she said, "Men don't change, Alicia. They never change."

The bitterness in her mom's voice was like a knife to her heart. Alicia rose to her feet too. "People do change. They grow, they apologize, they try to do better." She paused, but her mom wouldn't look at her. "Jeff's my *friend*, and if he ever comes over again, you need to treat him nicely. He's not the cause of our family's problems. Yeah, I was crushed when our friendship ended. But people change friends over the years. I moved on, and so should you."

Her mom shook her head. "It doesn't sound like you've moved on. He just brought you flowers."

Alicia closed her eyes for a moment. She wanted her friendship with Jeff to be a good thing in her life, not another stressful thing, and not something that would put a deeper wedge between her and her mom. But talking to her mom about it was like arguing in circles.

"I'll be back late tonight," Alicia said, changing the subject. "Friday nights we're open later than usual."

Her mom said nothing, and Alicia was at least grateful for the break in sarcastic comebacks. She went into her room to change into one of her black dresses that she rotated through for her hostess "uniform." This dress had a scooped neck and was longer than most of the others, but the slit on the left side came up to mid-thigh.

On impulse, she added a layer of eye-liner above her lashes and smoothed on a blush-pink lipstick called Kissable.

The makeup was more effort than her usual powder base and mascara, but knowing that Jeff would be bringing his lawyer for dinner at the restaurant meant that she'd probably be introduced. And she wanted to make a half-decent impression. Alicia had been able to get them a great table on the covered terrace that had a huge roaring hearth fire in the winter months. It would be perfect for the men. And it would also mean that Alicia wouldn't keep catching glimpses of them all night. Even though she'd argued with her mom about the flowers being completely friendly, Alicia's heart was starting to betray her. And she couldn't let that happen. Not with Jeff.

After one last check in the mirror, Alicia left her bedroom, locking the door behind her. Then she said goodbye to her mom, who mumbled something but didn't look up from her catalogs on the floor. Alicia slipped on her coat, then hurried outside into the fading winter light. The sunset was gorgeous with pink and orange splashes across the sky. She snapped a picture with her phone, then climbed into her cold car and started it up.

As she drove to the ski resort, she thought of the drive up here the day before when she'd spilled all her stress onto Jeff. He'd been a great listener, even though things were stressful in his own life. Yet, he'd spent the time to take her on a drive when it meant lost work hours. And then again last night . . . or early this morning . . . talking on the phone. After all that, he'd brought by flowers, only to be barraged by her mom. It was a wonder that Jeff had even answered his phone when she'd called him back. The least she could do was get him that reservation.

Twenty minutes later, she pulled into the restaurant parking lot and parked in the row that was designated for employees, which meant she had to walk a little farther in the cold. Her heels clicked as she walked, and she realized that her footsteps were lighter than usual. Something like happy anticipation buzzed through her.

By the time she reached the restaurant doors, she was smiling.

"Hey, you," Gwen said as Alicia walked in. "You're looking . . . sparkly."

"Sparkly?" Alicia said, slowing her step.

"Yeah, sparkly," Gwen said.

"If anyone's sparkly, it's you, blondie," Alicia said. Gwen's blonde hair was nearly platinum, and it was natural too. Although she was the most giving and selfless person Alicia knew, Gwen had a thing for beautiful fingernails. Every few days she changed the color and design. Tonight they were a light blue with plenty of glitter. She'd already made the change from her pink nails with Valentine hearts on them.

"Oh, you mean these?" Gwen said, holding up her hands and wiggling her fingers. "You've got to come with me to the nail salon one of these days. Bring your mom, too."

"We'll see," Alicia said. Gwen knew Alicia lived at home, but not under what circumstances.

"All right," Gwen said. "But you need to tell me what's going on. You've got the glowing skin going for you."

Alicia ignored that comment. "Do you need help setting up?" She looked past Gwen. The dinner hour would begin in about twenty minutes, so the restaurant was nearly empty, and a couple of the waiters were setting tables and folding napkins. Soon, the place would be filled with patrons.

Gwen grasped Alicia's arm before she could walk past. "It's got to be a guy. What's his name?"

Don't blush, Alicia commanded herself. She shook her head. "There's no guy."

Gwen brought a hand to her chin as if she was in deep thought. "That reservation you called in—Mr. Finch and Mr. Harris."

When Alicia couldn't hold back a blush, Gwen clapped her hands together. "You'd better dish, girlfriend. I want details."

"Ten minutes," the restaurant manager said, coming up to them. Seth Owens was maybe twenty-five, but he acted like he owned the place. In fact, his father did own the place, and Seth had been given free reign over the restaurant.

Gwen had worked here long before Seth, so she had plenty to complain about, but Alicia really had no issues with Seth. The restaurant was successful, things ran smoothly for the most part, and Alicia had gotten the schedule she wanted.

"We have some VIPs coming tonight," Seth continued, looking from Alicia to Gwen. He was a decent-looking guy, but too much of a pretty boy for Alicia. Besides, he was three years younger. When Seth wasn't managing the restaurant, he spent his time on the slopes, at least according to Gwen. And he was the ultimate ski bum. His blonde hair was darker than Gwen's and was always a bit unruly, like he kept it messy on purpose. But he wore expensive suits and always dressed immaculately—at least in the restaurant. "We need to make sure they enjoy their evening."

Gwen gave Seth her classic bored look.

Seth merely ignored it and kept talking. "Mr. and Mrs. Kensington are hosting the mayor and his press agent. We'll put them at table twenty-one."

"All right," Alicia said because Gwen didn't seem to want to contribute any sort of conversation with their boss. "What time will they be arriving?"

Seth's gaze shifted to Alicia, and she was struck by his

clear blue gaze—not like a ski bum at all. "Eight o' clock. I'll let you know if there's any delay."

"Very good." Alicia gave him a reassuring nod.

Gwen said nothing, even though Seth looked to her for confirmation.

Finally, something else caught his attention, and he moved past them.

"What's your problem with him?" Alicia asked Gwen when their boss was out of earshot.

"Besides the fact that I have to let some kid tell me how to do my job, and that I haven't had the raise I've put in a request for twice, I don't have any problem with him." Gwen rolled her eyes and walked away.

Alicia was annoyed that Gwen had brushed her off; but then again, Gwen had completely dropped the subject of why Alicia might be glowing. She put her hands to her cheeks— they weren't extra warm or anything. She couldn't dwell on Gwen's comments, or the fact that she'd be seeing Jeff in a couple of hours. So Alicia got busy, helping the waiters with the table arrangements, double checking all the reservations, and refilling the glass bowl with candied mints.

She wasn't surprised when her mom texted her, demanding that Alicia bring home "some of that fancy food." She wrote back, assuring her mom that she would, but to remember she wouldn't be home until nearly midnight. Her mom didn't respond to that.

Alicia sighed. She hoped she got her message through to her mom, and even if Jeff never did come to their house again, Alicia was glad that she'd faced the topic with her mom. Their therapist had told them to not let anything fester because that's when addictive behavior was exacerbated.

The first dinner patrons arrived at 5:45 p.m., and Alicia greeted them, then led them to their table. From then on, she was consistently busy, and so when Jeff arrived with another man, Alicia was surprised that it was 7:30 already.

Alicia felt an unwanted thrill run through her when Jeff came in through the doors. Their eyes locked, and then his gaze fell to her dress. Was he checking her out? Alicia smiled, ignoring the butterflies in her stomach. This was Jeff. Her friend. The man she didn't have a crush on.

Right behind Jeff was another man, who must be the lawyer, Mr. Harris, and wow, he looked like he'd stepped off a magazine photoshoot. What was it with Jeff's friends? Every inch of Mr. Harris seemed to exude power, and if Alicia put Jeff into the charming category, she'd put Mr. Harris into whatever category was above charming.

She was instinctively wary of Mr. Harris. His smile was brilliant when Jeff introduced his lawyer as Dawson Harris, and his handshake confident, yet lingering. When Alicia withdrew her hand from Dawson's, she felt as if she'd just ingested a five-hour energy drink. She had no doubt that Dawson was an excellent lawyer and always won his cases.

"This way, gentlemen," Alicia said, turning and leading them to their table.

Jeff walked close behind her, and Alicia thought of how different this was compared to when he'd come with his girlfriend. Seating Jeff with his lawyer was a much more pleasant task.

They sat down, and Alicia handed over their menus.

"Thanks again for working us in tonight," Jeff said, his ice-blue eyes holding her gaze and his mouth quirked into a half smile.

She would not blush. "You're most welcome. I'm glad you have something to celebrate."

"Jeff said this is the best restaurant in Pine Valley," Dawson said. "I can see what he meant."

Now she blushed. Dawson wasn't even checking her out, at least not that she could tell. Just the tone of his voice made her feel like he was. "Great. I hope you enjoy it. Our chef trained in Paris, although he's an expert at American cuisine as well."

Dawson smiled that brilliant smile of his.

Alicia tore her gaze from his and nodded at Jeff. "Can I get your drinks started? Your waitress will be here soon."

The men both ordered, and Alicia felt like she had to fan herself as she walked away. But she refrained. When she returned to the hostess stand, she closed her eyes for a moment to gather her wits.

"Wow." Gwen sidled up to her. "I get why you're glowing now."

"Please don't start anything," Alicia said.

Gwen folded her arms and stared Alicia down.

"All right, all right," Alicia said. "Jeff Finch is a high school friend, and Mr. Harris is his lawyer. They won a big case today, and they're here tonight to celebrate with dinner. Satisfied?"

Gwen smirked. "Mostly satisfied. So what's the story with Jeff Finch? He looked about ready to punch his lawyer in the face when you led them to their table."

"What do you mean?"

"It's obvious that the lawyer guy is just a player—probably charms every woman he meets—but Jeff Finch . . . He's protective of you. And you know what that means."

Alicia blinked. "And how do you know he's protective of me?"

"Well," Gwen said, leaning close to speak in a low voice as the front doors to the restaurant opened. "When I was bringing their drinks, I heard Jeff say to his friend, 'She's off-limits, Dawson. If you even think about asking her out, I'll be suing *you.*'"

Alicia's mouth dropped open.

"Like I said, *protective*," Gwen said with a wink, then turned and went back into the main restaurant.

Alicia didn't know what to think. And it was possible that Gwen was baiting her to get a reaction. She didn't have time to analyze what Jeff may or may not have said because a group of four was walking toward the hostess stand.

"Welcome to Alpine Lodge," she said, feeling like she was on auto-pilot. When she led the group of four to their table, she didn't even look toward the terrace to see how Jeff and Dawson were faring. She'd just have to trust Gwen to take care of them, and in the meantime, she needed to stop all the "what if" questions forming in her mind.

Twelve

Jeff laughed as Dawson told him a ridiculous story of one of his blind dates. Apparently, even high-powered lawyers got set up on blind dates by their mothers. "And this was a week after your divorce?" Jeff asked.

"No," Dawson said, shaking his head. "A week after Romy moved out. My mother was pretty excited to see her go, I guess."

"I guess," Jeff said, still chuckling. "Not even my mom is that brave."

"You've never been on a blind date?" Dawson asked, taking another sip of his wine.

"Nope." Jeff was the driver, so he wasn't drinking. This was also beneficial so he could keep his wits about him when he visited Paige later that night. She'd texted him several more times, begging for him to talk to her in person, and he'd finally told her he'd stop by after his dinner appointment.

"Meeting a woman on my own has always been better," Dawson said. "I mean, it should be better." He spread his hands. "Yet . . . no girlfriend, no wife, maybe I *am* doing something wrong."

Jeff shrugged. "I'm not doing much better."

"So what happened with Paige?" Dawson asked.

Jeff took another bite of the sautéed asparagus, stalling. "Some women are beautiful on the outside, but not so much on the inside, if you know what I mean."

"Yeah, I do," Dawson said. "I married one of those." He looked past Jeff. "Alicia isn't like that though, is she?"

When Dawson refocused his gaze on Jeff, it was his lawyer, don't-lie-to-me gaze.

"No, she's not," Jeff said. "Like I told you, we've been friends since we were kids, and she is one of the good ones. Too good for you, that's for sure." He spoke in a light tone, but he also gave Dawson his own don't-mess-with-her-gaze.

"I got it the first time," Dawson said, narrowing his eyes. "She's not just a friend, is she? I mean, you're not thinking of her as a little sister you're watching out for, are you?"

"I don't have a sister."

"Exactly." Dawson tapped the table. "You've been friends forever, so what's the delay?"

"What delay would that be?" Jeff said in a stubborn tone. He wasn't going to admit anything, not to himself or to Dawson.

Dawson leaned forward. "Why haven't you asked her out? I mean, it's pretty clear that you're into her way more than 'as a friend.'"

Jeff rubbed at his neck; he was too hot. "It's a long story. But the end of that long story is that I'd never push anything onto her. She's not someone I'd ever want to hurt."

Dawson nodded thoughtfully. "Who says you'd be pushing yourself onto her? Even a blind man could see the tension between the two of you."

Jeff reached for his ice water and downed the rest of it. "The tension isn't what you think it is."

"Oh?" Dawson's eyes brightened. "Enlighten me, my friend."

So, Jeff did. He told Dawson the whole story with most of the sordid details. He left out the issues that Alicia had with her mom, and he didn't mention the flower incident. But by the time he'd finished, Jeff had told Dawson more about Alicia than he'd ever told anyone.

Dawson blew out a breath. "I really didn't expect that." Another swallow of his wine. "You're right, man. She's off limits to me. But I think you're in real danger of making a complete fool of yourself over her."

"Why do you say that?" Jeff asked.

"It takes a long time for a woman to forgive a man who treated her like dirt," Dawson said, his tone knowledgeable. "Believe me, I know. I don't think Romy will ever let me live some stuff down." He poured more wine and took several long swallows.

"Good thing I'm driving," Jeff observed in a dry tone.

"Talking about my ex-wife seems to bring out the best in me." Dawson finished off the wine in his glass and poured another. "And since it sounds like Alicia's well on her way to forgiving you, I can see that you've already fallen hard."

"You've had way too much wine to make any sort of assessment. I haven't fallen for her." Jeff moved the bottle of wine out of Dawson's reach. He wasn't going to let the man get too drunk. "We're friends, that's all. Friends who go a long way back." How many times did he have to point this out?

Dawson looked at the wine bottle for a moment, then refocused on Jeff. "And you just happened to break up with your girlfriend hours after seeing Alicia for the first time in ten years?"

"That was a pure coincidence," Jeff said, although he wondered if Dawson was right—at least on that point. Not on any of the others, of course. Seeing Alicia had reminded Jeff of how difficult his relationship with Paige was, and how exhausting it had been to keep her happy. The difference with Alicia was that he wanted to be her friend, wanted to spend time with her, wanted to help her in any way he could.

"Would you fellows like to see the dessert menu?" the waitress asked, coming back to their table.

Jeff recognized her as Gwen, the woman who was a friend to Alicia.

"I'm fine," Jeff said, then looked at Dawson. "What about you?"

"No, I'm full," Dawson said, his eyes on Gwen. "And besides, looking at you is dessert enough."

Jeff groaned. "Sorry about that," he said to Gwen. "He's had too much wine."

Gwen smiled sweetly, but her eyes weren't so sweet. "That's okay. The only reason I'm not going to double your drink bill is because you know Alicia. But if your friend ever comes back, I'll make sure he gets charged premium prices." She slapped the bill folder on the table and walked away.

"Ouch," Dawson said, rubbing a hand over his face. "I think I drank too much."

"You think? Weren't you just talking about how we should treat people?" Jeff pulled out two one-hundred-dollar bills and put them into the bill folder. "Let's get out of here before you get us kicked out."

Dawson rose to his feet, using the table to keep his balance. "I need to find her and apologize."

"No, we need to leave." Jeff moved toward him and grasped Dawson's arm.

Dawson nodded. "All right. Maybe your friend can tell her."

"Maybe," Jeff said, in a noncommittal tone.

They walked through the restaurant, with Jeff on alert in case Dawson did or said something else stupid. But the man stayed subdued. Alicia wasn't at the hostess stand when they passed by, and Jeff glanced about for her, but he didn't want to wait around. The sooner he got Dawson in the SUV, and home, the better.

By the time Jeff dropped off Dawson at his condo, the man was nearly asleep. He watched Dawson unlock his door and flip on some lights. *Good enough,* Jeff decided. He pulled out of the parking lot, then drove to Paige's apartment. He didn't want to be on her turf, but he wanted this over, and he hoped this would be the last time he'd have to see her.

When he knocked on the door, it opened almost immediately. Had she seen him pull into the parking lot?

"Come in, babe," Paige said in a sweet voice—one Jeff didn't trust for a moment.

She wore a silky white robe, and her blonde hair was piled on top of her head, as if she were just lounging around her place late at night. But he didn't miss the fact that her makeup was immaculate, and she even wore red lipstick. Music played in the background, and several candles had been lit in the front room. Paige always liked candles.

He took a step back. "Hey, it's late, and I thought we could maybe meet for coffee in the morning."

"Oh, no you don't," Paige said, grasping his hand and tugging him inside the apartment.

But Jeff held his ground. He stayed by the front door. "Look, I'm not here for this." He waved his hand toward the set of candles.

Paige pushed her lips into a pout. "This? I'm just reading,

you idiot. You know I love candles. Chill out and come in. I deserve better than an argument on the phone. Plus, it's freezing outside."

"I wasn't trying to argue with you on the phone," Jeff said. "I told you I wanted to talk in person, but you forced me to explain why over the phone."

Paige folded her arms, and Jeff didn't miss how sheer the fabric of her robe really was.

"Okay, then let's talk," she said. "That's all I want to do. You really shouldn't flatter yourself, Jeff Finch." She reached past him and shut the door.

At least she didn't lock it, and Jeff took courage in that. He walked to one of the stuffed chairs and sat down. "Look, I'm sorry for how everything's played out, but like I said, things haven't been going very well between us for weeks."

Paige didn't say anything. She picked up a water bottle from the coffee table and took a long swallow. Then she turned to him and held it out. "Thirsty?"

"No, thanks," Jeff said. *Just sit down so we can get this over with,* he wanted to tell her.

Paige released a sigh, then walked toward him. "I hate it when you're mad at me."

"Paige," Jeff said, his sharp tone stopping her advance. "I'm not mad at you, but we're over. I'm really sorry."

"I'm really sorry I had to bail early on our Valentine's date," Paige said as if she hadn't heard a word he'd spoken. She untied her robe and let the silky fabric slide from her shoulders.

Jeff blinked. She wore a white negligee that was completely transparent. Before he could react, she straddled his lap and wrapped her arms about his neck.

"Don't be mad, baby," she said, then pressed her mouth against his.

Jeff had frozen, in shock or disbelief, or both. His hands moved to her hips as she kissed him. He might be a man, and she might be a beautiful, very tempting woman, but this wasn't happening. He gripped her hips and lifted her off his lap.

"Oh, that's better. Carry me to the bedroom," Paige said with a giggle.

Jeff stood with her still clinging to him, and it took more effort than he imagined to peel her off of him. "I'm leaving now. Don't call me or text me." He strode to the door and tugged it open.

"Don't you dare walk out on me," Paige yelled. "You're cheating on me, aren't you?"

Jeff hurried down the walkway, then cut across the yard, ignoring the snow that would soak his shoes and socks. The short cut was more than worth it.

Apparently Paige wasn't done yet. She came out of her apartment, gracing whoever cared to look out their windows with her attire. Her voice went up a notch on the hysterical scale. "If you leave, I'm never taking you back! No matter how much you beg. I can find a new man tomorrow if I want. Or tonight! You're a loser, do you hear me, a—"

Jeff started the engine and roared out of the parking lot, drowning out her screeches. If her neighbors were smart, they'd call the cops. He slammed his hand against the steering wheel. How did he get himself attached to someone like Paige? He was done making stupid decisions with women. He shouldn't date anyone for a long time, maybe a year.

By the time he reached his house and pulled into the garage, his breathing had calmed down, but he was still angry at himself. He knew what Paige was when he'd met her.

Jeff climbed out of his SUV and shut the garage door. Inside his house, he left all the lights off and made his way to the living room, where he sat on the couch. The blinds were open, and the pale moonlight filtered across the floor in stripes.

He closed his eyes and exhaled. Then he pulled out his phone and stared at it. There had been no message from Alicia. Surely she was off work by now. He sent a text, hoping that she wasn't mad at him or anything. *I didn't get a chance to say goodbye. I was hoping to talk to you about Gwen.*

The text was delivered and read, but there was no return reply. *That's okay,* Jeff told himself. It had been one crazy day, and it was time for it to end. Court, being chewed out by Mrs. Waters, dinner with his drunk lawyer, then Paige . . . Jeff turned off his phone and plugged it in. Then he changed and climbed into bed. Sleep didn't come for a long time, but at least tomorrow would be a new day.

Thirteen

*L*ast night, Alicia had seen the moment Jeff's text had come in. It had been nearly midnight, and she decided to not reply yet. She'd heard about what his lawyer had said to Gwen, and she was glad that Jeff had stuck up for Gwen. But it also reminded Alicia of why she hated the dating scene. Why did some guys think that making sexual comments toward a woman would make them interested, or heaven forbid, secure them a date?

Gwen had been livid, and when she told Alicia, Alicia had to take her into the kitchen to calm her down. Alicia knew how much Gwen needed her job, and if she let one customer who was a jerk ruin the rest of the night, they might have even more problems. So Alicia hadn't seen Jeff and Dawson leave, and that was probably a good thing.

Ironically, it was their manager, Seth Owens, who had been able to talk Gwen off the ledge, and she'd gone back to work.

Now, it was nearly 5:00 p.m., and Alicia had just pulled

up to the restaurant to start her shift. There hadn't been any more texts from Jeff, and Alicia felt bad about still not responding, but she wanted to see how Gwen was doing first. If Gwen was all right, then Alicia might be able to call Jeff without cursing out his lawyer.

Gwen was at the hostess stand, writing down reservations, when Alicia entered. Gwen looked up, and Alicia was glad to see that her friend was clear-eyed and looked fine.

"How are you?" Alicia asked.

Gwen shrugged. "Fine. Why do you ask?"

"Well, considering you almost quit your job last night, I just wondered." Alicia winked.

"Well . . ." Gwen echoed. "I actually need to thank Mr. Dawson Harris if I ever see him again."

"What?" Alicia couldn't be more surprised.

"Apparently our boss has a protective quirk for his employees, and he told me he was approving the raise I requested," Gwen said with a grin.

"Oh, wow, that's great," Alicia said. "I guess that's a nice consolation prize?"

"It doesn't excuse Mr. Harris's behavior, but honestly, I've heard much worse," she said. "I guess I was just extra moody last night. Who would have thought? Moodiness works on our boss."

"*Works* on him?" Alicia asked. "What else are you trying to get out of him?"

Gwen pursed her lips, raised her brows, then turned and walked away.

"Gwen? That's not fair," Alicia called after her. "You can't leave me hanging."

But Gwen had disappeared into the kitchen. Shaking her head, Alicia started to look over the reservations for that night. Her gaze skipped over the list, searching for a name she knew, which she always did out of habit. No Jeff Finch, or anyone else that she knew was coming tonight.

The front doors opened, and Alicia looked up, expecting to see one of the waiters or kitchen staff arriving. Instead, the blond man who stepped inside was unexpected.

"Dawson? What are you doing here?" Alicia said, before she could stop herself.

"I, uh, Jeff told me that I could find Gwen here—and you," Dawson said, coming in. He was still dressed to the nines, but his confidence seemed about ten levels lower than it had last night. "I needed to make an apology."

Alicia folded her arms. "I don't think it's a good idea for you to come here."

"Please hear me out," Dawson said, raising a hand. "I know I was a jerk, and even though I'd had too much wine, that's no excuse. I wanted to apologize last night, but Jeff hauled me out of here. Which was probably a good thing."

Alicia nodded. She could agree with that.

"Please, can you tell Gwen I'm here?" Dawson said. "Let her decide if she wants to talk to me."

Alicia exhaled. "All right. But if she doesn't want to talk to you, and you refuse to leave, I'm calling security."

"Okay, okay," Dawson said, shoving his hands in his pockets. "Believe me, I get it."

Alicia turned and strode to the kitchen. Inside, Gwen was chatting with one of the other waiters. Their chef was chopping greens, and their manager was training a newer waiter on the cash register machine.

When Alicia told Gwen that Dawson Harris was in the front foyer, their manager came over.

"It's all right," Gwen said, looking from Alicia to Seth. "I'll talk to the man. He can give his apology, then leave."

"I'm coming with you," Seth told her.

She raised her brows in surprise, but Alicia could see that she was pleased. "I'll be fine."

"Because I'll make sure of it," he continued.

Gwen shrugged. "All right." She walked out of the kitchen, with Seth and Alicia following.

Dawson looked up when the group of them came into the foyer. If he was surprised, he didn't show it.

"Hi," Dawson said. "I came to apologize for what I said last night."

Gwen stopped a few steps from him, her arms folded. "Bad day, and too much wine? Decided to take it out on me?"

"Not exactly," Dawson said, looking from Gwen to Seth. "It was actually a decent day, and I did have too much to drink, but I'm not usually such a jerk, drunk or not."

No one spoke for a moment.

"So, you're not going to give me a pitiful excuse?" Gwen said, her expression softening.

Seth's expression was still hard.

"No excuse, just an apology," Dawson said. "I'd love to make it up to you."

Gwen lifted an eyebrow. "Make it up to me? How would you do that?"

Dawson hesitated, glancing again at Seth. "Dinner?"

Gwen laughed, then she stepped forward and tapped Dawson on the chest. "Nice try. But no thank you." She turned and walked back to the kitchen, still laughing.

Alicia stared after her. Then she looked at Dawson, who seemed stunned that his offer of a date had been turned down.

"Mr. Harris," Seth said, drawing Dawson's complete attention. "You're banned from this restaurant for six months. If I need to get a restraining order, I will."

Dawson narrowed his eyes. "Who are you?"

"Seth Owens, owner and manager."

Dawson nodded. "You won't need a restraining order." He took a couple of steps back. "My apologies to all of you." And then he turned and pushed through the restaurant doors.

"Well," Alicia said, looking over at Seth.

"How do I know that guy?" Seth asked.

"He's a big-deal attorney," Alicia said. "In the newspaper a lot."

Seth nodded. "Ah, that's probably it." He walked away, shaking his head and muttering, "It's about time the tables were turned on him."

But Alicia couldn't help but smile. Gwen had actually liked Seth coming to her rescue even though she probably wouldn't admit it. And Alicia was glad Dawson had come to apologize in person. She'd probably cross paths with him again, and she didn't want things to be awkward. All of this reminded her that she should probably text back Jeff.

I'm at work, and Dawson just came in to apologize to Gwen. Then he tried to ask her out.

Jeff replied almost instantly. *Really? I hope she turned him down. And I'm sorry for what he said last night. I was so pissed at him.*

Alicia wrote: *She did turn him down. LOL. And he's lucky to have you for a friend.*

So, are we still friends?

Alicia didn't hesitate. *Yep.*

Jeff texted back an emoji with heart eyes, and Alicia tried not to read too much into it, although her heart was doing a weird pounding thing.

The restaurant doors opened again, and a waitress walked in. "Hi, Ellie," Alicia said.

"Sorry I'm late, is Mr. Owens already here?"

"He is," Alicia said. "But you're not that late."

Ellie nodded, her long black pony-tail swinging as she did so. She hurried past Alicia and entered the kitchen. As she opened the door, Gwen came out and joined Alicia at the hostess stand.

"Who would have thought Owen is the manager and owner of the restaurant?" Gwen said in a conspiratorial tone.

"Is he really? Or was he just chest-pounding in front of Dawson?" Alicia asked.

"Oh, I confronted him," Gwen said with a wink. "I'm sort of on a roll this weekend. I asked him point blank, and he said that he owns 65% of the restaurant. So there you go."

"So not only is he your knight in shining armor, but he's your wealthy knight in shining armor," Alicia said with a laugh.

"Ha." Gwen jabbed at Alicia's shoulder. "You know how I feel about rich people. They're no better than my homeless friends. Rich people just have a permanent roof over their heads."

"True."

"And how's Jeff Finch doing?" Gwen asked. "Are you going out this weekend?"

"We're friends, I told you," Alicia said. "Besides, I don't date. Not with my schedule." And she wasn't really interested in trying to keep a relationship together when her mom was still doing poorly. And who knew how long that would last.

"So it's still off limits to set you up?" Gwen asked.

"Yep." Alicia waved her away. "Don't you have something to do? Like go talk to our boss, or something?"

"Very funny," Gwen said with a smirk. But she walked away, leaving Alicia to her own thoughts.

Gwen had tried to set her up on a couple of dates, but Alicia had always turned her down, even the double dates. She knew too many people in Pine Valley—or at least did in high school— and the last thing she wanted was for someone to ask about her mom.

When the first patrons came into the restaurant, Alicia seated them, then returned to the hostess stand. The night was pretty mellow, even boring, without the anticipation of seeing Jeff coming in for dinner. As the hours dragged, Alicia was surprised that her mom hadn't texted any orders. So during a down time, Alicia wrote: *Any special requests from the restaurant?*

An hour later, there was no reply. On her next break, Alicia called her mom's phone. It rang several times, but she didn't answer. That meant the phone wasn't off at least. Alicia kept trying to call, getting more and more nervous as time slipped by.

"Are you okay?" Gwen asked, stopping by the hostess stand a little after 9:00 p.m.

Alicia flinched.

"Whoa, what's going on?"

"Just worried about my mom," Alicia said. "Long story, but I can usually get ahold of her. She hasn't answered her phone all night."

Gwen frowned. "Maybe she lost it or put it on silent."

Shaking her head, Alicia said, "No. I'm just hoping she's asleep or something." This wasn't the place to go into personal stuff about her mom.

"Things are slow tonight," Gwen said. "I can see if Seth will let you go home early."

Alicia exhaled. "That would be great."

Gwen gave her a quick smile. "Be right back."

Fifteen minutes later, Alicia was in her car, driving home. She hated to cut out on work, but she had to find out if her mom was okay. The worst-case scenarios kept running through her mind as she drove. When she pulled up to the house, the place was dark. This wasn't good. Her mom always kept lights on, even if she was going to bed.

Alicia jumped out of the car and hurried to the front door. It was unlocked, another thing that made her worried. She pushed open the door. "Mom?" she said into the darkness as dread shot through her. Something wasn't right. She flipped on a light. "Mom?" Then her phone rang, and Alicia's heart skipped. Hopefully it was her mom. But the number said UNKNOWN. Alicia hesitated. Should she answer it or not? Finally, she answered it.

"Hello?"

"Alicia?"

Alicia's knees nearly gave. "Mom, where are you?" She shut the door against the cold.

"I'm at the police station," she said. "You need to bring down six hundred twenty-five dollars in exact change for the bail money and get me out of here."

"What? What happened? Are you all right?"

"I didn't do anything," her mom said. "I was just walking in the neighborhood, and the neighbor decided to call the cops. When I tried to explain, the cops wouldn't listen. They just handcuffed me and brought me here."

Alicia didn't know whether to cry or yell at her mom. "What were you doing? People don't just call the cops if nothing is going on. Did you get into someone's garbage can?"

"I wasn't doing anything wrong," her mom insisted, her voice getting higher pitched. "Our neighbor is a jerk. Go get the money."

Alicia glanced at the clock on the living room wall. No banks were open this time of night. Besides, her debit card would only pull out three hundred at a time. She scrambled for her purse and pulled out her wallet. She only had a five-dollar bill. "Do you have any cash? Or where's your debit card?"

"The cops took my bag, and they won't give it back," her mom said. The phone beeped. "Hurry." Then the line was disconnected.

Alicia stared at her phone, trying to not let the tears come. Her mom had been arrested again. Now she'd have a record. She'd have to go to court. Get a lawyer. How much would that all cost? Tears burned in Alicia's eyes no matter how much she wanted to stay calm. Maybe she could go to the gas station and buy something, then request cash back. She hurried out of the house, locked the door, and jumped in her still-warm car. After she pulled out her limit at the bank, she drove to the gas station. Thankfully it was still open.

"Hi," she said to the pimple-faced young man at the cash register as she handed over a bag of M&Ms. "I need this and to get cash back."

"Sure," the young man said, ringing her up.

The card swipe machine gave her a choice of twenty or forty dollars. "Can I request more than forty dollars?"

"Nope," the cashier said. "Forty's the limit. We don't keep a lot of cash on hand. Helps keep the thieves away."

"Can I do more than one transaction, then?" she asked.

The cashier shrugged. "You can try."

Alicia swiped her card. *Denied.* She swiped it again.

"Do you have another card?" the cashier asked, his bored expression telling her that this happened quite often.

"No," Alicia said.

"Well, you'll have to call your bank then."

Alicia pulled up her banking app. She should have enough money in there, but when she saw her balance she realized that her most current paycheck was still showing as "pending" and she couldn't withdraw on it yet.

She closed her eyes; she was out of ideas.

"Are you okay?" the cashier asked.

Alicia opened her eyes. "Sorry. It's just been a bad night. Thanks." She left the M&M's on the counter and walked out of the gas station, feeling both mortified and angry. By the time she got to her car and climbed in, the tears had started again. "Stupid, stupid, stupid." Why couldn't her mom stay home? Why did she have to look through other people's trash? Wasn't ordering junk online enough to keep her happy? Even if Alicia called her dad, what would he do? He couldn't bring her cash in the middle of the night. He lived over two hours away.

She could call Gwen, but she was probably still at work. Or Jeff.

Alicia sighed, her stomach twisting as she pulled up Jeff's number. Hopefully he wasn't on a date with someone. Hopefully this wasn't jumping the boundaries of their new friendship.

Fourteen

Jeff had been dead asleep when his phone rang. Apparently the crazy week had finally caught up with him. It took him a few seconds to clear the fog from his brain and register that Alicia was calling him. He glanced at the digital clock on his bed: 11:00 p.m.

"Hello?" he said, his voice hoarse with sleep. He cleared his throat. "Alicia?"

"Jeff?"

In that one word, he heard the distress in her voice. He sat up, scrubbing a hand through his hair. "Are you okay?"

"My mom's in jail," she said in a trembling voice.

It took several seconds for him to process what she'd said. "*Jail?* What happened?" And then in a tearful voice, she told him about her mom not being home, and then calling from the jail and saying she'd been arrested. Jeff understood about half of what she said through her crying.

"Where are you?" Jeff asked, rising from the bed and looking for his shoes. He'd fallen asleep in his clothes. "I'll meet you."

"I'm at the gas station by my neighborhood. I was trying to get some money, but my bank won't let me pull out more than three hundred at a time, and my paycheck is still pending."

Jeff stilled. "How much is the bail?"

"Six twenty-five, exact change. I have three hundred five right now."

"Okay." He exhaled. "I'll bring the rest and pick you up at your house."

Her voice sounded very small when she said, "All right."

"Alicia, it will be fine, I promise. Go home and wait for me there. I'm on my way." When he hung up with Alicia, he pulled on his shoes, grabbed his wallet and coat, then headed into the garage. He felt like he was in a dream. But this was no dream. Alicia needed his help.

As he drove, he could only hope that Mrs. Waters would learn her lesson, that she would use this experience and start to change. On the other hand, he was mad that a neighbor called the cops instead of just talking to her—at least, he assumed that's what had happened. People didn't talk to each other nowadays. They either texted to communicate or just called the cops. This was a sixty-year-old mentally ill woman, for heaven's sake.

Jeff was tempted to call Dawson on the way, but then he changed his mind. Jeff wouldn't know all the answers to the questions Dawson was likely to ask. Tonight, he'd focus on helping Alicia and her mom, and tomorrow they could figure out what the damage was and how to fix it.

Alicia was standing on the porch when he pulled up, shivering in her coat. She was still wearing high heels— probably from work. And she looked beautiful in a sort of forlorn, tragic way.

Jeff jumped out of the SUV, his heart going out to her. He strode toward her as she stepped off the porch. "Ready?"

She nodded, and he could see her swollen eyes from the light of the porch.

"Hey, we'll get her out of there and figure out what to do." He wrapped his arms about her shoulders, and she leaned into him, moving her arms about his waist. Her cheek was cold; her hair was even cold.

She pulled away after a few seconds, and said, "I'm freezing."

"Let's go get your mom, then." He opened the passenger door of the SUV for her, then hurried to climb into the driver's side. He pulled out the cash he'd brought to add to the bail and handed it over. "Here's three-twenty."

Alicia took the money. "Thanks so much for this. I'll pay you back tomorrow. And I'm sorry for waking you up."

"I don't normally fall asleep that early," Jeff said, backing out of the driveway, then pulling onto the road. "Don't worry, I'm always up for a little adventure."

Alicia scoffed. "Adventures to the city jailhouse?"

He shrugged and looked over at her with a smile. At least she wasn't crying anymore. "This kind of stuff is always better to go through with a friend, right?"

"Right," Alicia said, looking at him. "You should really keep a box of tissues in here if we're going to be friends."

"Good idea," Jeff said with a laugh.

When she went quiet again, he said, "Are you okay?"

"Yeah," she said in a soft voice. "I just wish I hadn't waited ten years to start hanging out with you again."

Warmth buzzed through Jeff. "Why's that?"

"Well, none of my other friends would have picked me up in the middle of the night and given me a wad of cash."

Jeff liked that she was teasing him. He grabbed her hand, purely on impulse, and brought it to his mouth to kiss it. She didn't pull away, so he continued to hold it until he had to pull into the parking lot of the police station. This was one place in Pine Valley where the lights stayed on all night.

"I wonder if Leo is on duty tonight," Jeff said, putting the SUV in park and turning off the engine.

"Leo Russo?"

"Yeah, he's a cop now."

"I didn't know," Alicia said in a slow voice. "Wasn't he the kid who always got put in detention for pulling the fire alarm?"

Jeff laughed. "Yep. One and the same. I guess life's a full circle."

"Who would have thought?"

Although she'd stopped crying and seemed to be talking normally, he still sensed the nervous tension in her as they pushed through the station's front doors. They went through the security check, and he walked with her to the front reception desk.

"I'm here to pay bail for my mom," Alicia said in a breathless voice.

"I need to see your ID, please," the female officer at the desk said.

Alicia handed it over, and while they waited, Jeff looked about the lobby area. "Is Officer Russo around tonight?"

The woman at the desk looked up. "He is. Do you want me to call him?"

"Sure," Jeff said, casting a glance at Alicia. He didn't know if talking to Leo would help the situation or not, but he could only try.

Alicia finished paying, and the female officer picked up

her phone. "Lila Waters is being released. Bring her to the lobby." Then she punched in another number. "Leo Russo, you have visitors."

Moments later, Leo Russo arrived. "Jeff Finch," he said, sticking out his hand. He still had the same easygoing smile as he'd had in high school, but he'd bulked up considerably over the years—probably due to police training. He caught sight of Alicia. "Alicia Waters? Is that you?"

"Yep," she said.

Leo's smile was wary. "What brings the both of you here?"

Jeff was about to answer, but Alicia said, "My mom was arrested tonight. A neighbor called the cops on her for going through their garbage or something. I'd like to see the police report."

Leo's brows shot up. "I didn't know she was your mom," he said. "I should have recognized her name."

Alicia shrugged. "It's not like we knew each other's parents in high school."

"Right." Leo looked from Alicia to Jeff, a question in his eyes. "I can't release the report until it's been filed."

"Can you do us this one favor so we know what really happened, and what we're dealing with?" Jeff said in a low voice. He was glad Leo was sticking to the rules, but waiting would only make the whole situation more stressful. Plus, he wanted to give Dawson a call as soon as they got Alicia's mom home.

"Sorry, no can do," Leo said, rocking back on his heels. "I'll push it through first thing in the morning, if that helps."

Jeff clenched his jaw but answered in an even tone. "Thanks, man. That will help." He looked at Alicia. "Do you want to give him your email so he can send it to you?"

"Sure," Alicia said. She scrambled for something to write on in her purse and handed over a receipt with her email written on it.

"Do you have a direct number we can reach you at?" Jeff asked, pulling out his phone.

"Sure, but I wasn't the arresting officer," Leo said.

"That's all right," Jeff said. "I'd rather go through you."

Leo rattled off his number, and Jeff put it in his phone.

Just then, Mrs. Waters was led out by a female officer. She was wearing a coat over dark sweat pants and a purple sweater. At least she wasn't wearing the ratty bathrobe Jeff had seen her in the other day. Her hair hung about her face as if she hadn't washed or brushed it for weeks. The dark circles under her eyes told Jeff that Alicia's mom was in her own personal hell.

He watched as she approached Alicia, and said, "Did you pay the bail?"

"Yes, Mom," Alicia said. "Are you okay?"

Her mom scowled. "No. I'm in jail! How do you think I am?"

Jeff winced.

"Let's get you home, and you can tell us what happened," Alicia said with a sigh.

"I'll tell you what happened," her mom said, not moving. "I was going on a walk, and our idiot neighbor called the cops on me. No one would listen, they just wanted my money."

"Okay, Mom, let's go," Alicia said, grasping her mom's arm.

Remarkably the woman didn't pull away. It seemed her bark was stronger than her bite.

"You can sit in the front," Alicia said, leading her to the SUV and opening the passenger door.

"What's this? Where did you get this car?" her mom asked.

"It's Jeff's," Alicia said. "He drove me."

Her mom looked over at Jeff, her eyes widening as if she'd just noticed him for the first time. Perhaps she had. "Why did *he* drive you? What's wrong with your car? Did you forget to change the oil again?"

"That was when I was sixteen, mom," Alicia said. "Just get in the SUV. It's freezing out here."

This time the irritation in her voice was plain, Jeff noted. But it seemed that as stubborn as Mrs. Waters was, Alicia was more stubborn. Her mom finally climbed into the SUV.

Jeff climbed in, too, and started up the heater on full blast. He decided to let Alicia carry the conversation; Mrs. Waters had already put him in his place.

As he drove back to their house, Mrs. Waters cast him a few glances. Jeff kept driving, not saying anything.

"I'm getting the police report tomorrow," Alicia said. "But I want to know why you got arrested. What were you doing?"

Mrs. Waters threw her hands up. "Nothing. I was on a walk, that's all."

"Did you go into someone's yard?" Alicia said.

"I was just making sure the Osbournes weren't throwing away anything that could still be used," her mom said. "You wouldn't believe what people throw away."

"Mom, you can't go onto someone else's property and look through their garbage," Alicia said. "That's like going into their house and stealing."

Mrs. Waters scoffed. "That's where you're wrong. It's called *garbage* for a reason. They don't want it anymore."

"It's illegal," Alicia said. "Even if you did that at the gas station, you'd be cited."

"It's ridiculous," her mom said, not budging on her defense. "The cops have nothing better to do, and the

Osbournes have no business throwing away a perfectly good lamp. They could have at least donated it to Goodwill."

Alicia sighed. "Was it worth $625? And for me and Jeff to come and pick you up in the middle of the night? Not to mention whatever court dates you have to go to now. And what about lawyer fees?"

"I'm not paying for a lawyer," her mom said, her chin jutting up. "If they want me in court, then *they* can pay for the lawyer."

Jeff was about to drive Mrs. Waters back to the station. He didn't know how Alicia could be so patient with her mom. It was like arguing with a teenager. When he pulled into the driveway, Mrs. Waters unbuckled her seatbelt and opened the door before he'd come to a full stop.

"Mom," Alicia said, exasperation in her voice.

Her mom slammed the door and stalked to the house.

"I'm so sorry," Alicia told Jeff, her voice trembling. "She drives me crazy, and now I've dragged you into this. I mean, I just bailed her out of jail, and she's angry at *me*."

Jeff reached back and grabbed her hand. "Let me help. I'll talk to her." He didn't know why he was offering, but maybe having a different person than Alicia try to talk sense into her would help.

Alicia hesitated. "I don't know. She can be pretty cruel."

"If she gets too upset, I can leave," Jeff said. "But I want to tell her what little I know about the court system and maybe even talk to her about getting a lawyer. I'm hoping this will be a wake-up call for her."

"Me too," Alicia said, squeezing his hand, then letting go. "She won't be happy that I'm letting you inside the house."

"I can handle it."

"It's pretty awful in there," Alicia continued. "Just know that my room is immaculate."

"Of course it is," Jeff said. Although his tone was light, he didn't want her to think that he was going to judge Alicia by her mom's actions. Besides, how bad could a few piles of junk be?

They both climbed out of the SUV, and as they approached the house, it looked like Mrs. Waters had turned on every single light.

"She likes the lights on," Alicia said. "At first, I thought it was because she hated the dark, but the therapist told me it's because the visual sight of all of her stuff reduces her anxiety levels."

Alicia opened the door and stepped inside the house. Jeff walked in behind her, thinking he'd face a familiar sight. He'd been inside the Waters house plenty when he was a kid. At first, he thought he'd stepped into a warehouse, but there was carpet, a couch, and a rocking chair. He'd heard of hoarding, of course, but had never actually witnessed it.

One wall was lined with bookcases, stuffed with books and other odds and ends. On the side of the front door and running toward what must be the kitchen were stacked boxes, two or three deep. The hallway that led to the bedrooms was shrunk down to a narrow passageway because of the number of boxes. It looked as if someone had just moved in or was getting ready to move.

Since the light in the kitchen was on as well, he could see that the counters were stacked with dishes, towels, and kitchen gadgets. On the kitchen table sat a wooden crate that was filled with picture frames; on top of the frames were two toasters that looked like they'd seen better days.

"What's he doing here?" Mrs. Waters asked.

Jeff swung his gaze toward the gas fireplace where she stood. He hadn't even noticed her there at first. She was holding her hands out to the flames. Next to her was a coffee table with stacks of magazines and catalogs that would rival any library's collection.

Mrs. Waters didn't look happy with his presence, and he could only hope that she'd listen to him. She had to listen to someone.

Fifteen

Alicia held her breath as Jeff and her mom gazed at each other. Not only was Alicia cringing over the fact that Jeff was actually in her house and a front-row witness to the disaster that was their home, but her mom looked ready to pounce.

"I have a lawyer friend who can help you with whatever the cops are going to charge you with," Jeff said. "Can I have him call you tomorrow?"

Alicia looked to her mom, surprised that she wasn't immediately turning Jeff down. "All right. He can call me at 11:00 tomorrow morning. I like to sleep in a little."

Jeff nodded, and relief swept through Alicia. She couldn't guess what was going through his mind right now, and she wouldn't blame him if he left and never knocked on her door again.

"Great. His name is Dawson Harris," Jeff said. "He helped me with some important legal matters recently, so I highly recommend him."

Her mom narrowed her eyes. "Alicia said you'd been to court. How much does this lawyer cost?"

"Turns out he owes me a couple of favors," Jeff said with a smile that Alicia was sure he didn't truly feel. "So there won't be any charge for him to help you."

At this, her mom seemed to be impressed. "All right, then. Eleven o' clock, but no earlier."

"Great," Jeff said. "Also, I wondered if you've ever made jewelry. Each week, my mom does orders for an Etsy company. She makes earrings and bracelets, and she's always looking for help."

Alicia stared at Jeff, but he was focused on her mom.

"Jewelry?" her mom said.

"Yeah, it pays pretty well, too," Jeff said. "You can do it at home, and then my mom can pick up the finished pieces and mail them for you. Or Alicia can mail them. What do you think?"

Her mom shrugged.

Jeff pulled out his phone, then walked over to her mom. "Here's a picture of some of the jewelry my mom made."

Her mom peered at the picture that Jeff showed her. "Those are pretty. How much do the materials cost?"

Alicia couldn't believe her mom was interested in this. She would have never guessed.

"No cost to you," Jeff said. "My mom would just bring over the materials, you make them, and then you get paid as soon as they are shipped. It's all automatic and comes into whichever account you want it to."

Her mom glanced at Alicia, and she recognized the calculating look on her mom's face. She was probably trying to figure out if she could make decent money.

"It's up to you," Jeff continued. "My mom loves it, and she can make as much or as little money as she wants. She can do it at home while she watches TV or listens to an audio book. Should I have her call you?"

Her mom shrugged. "Your mom was always nice to me. I remember those cinnamon rolls she used to make."

Jeff laughed. "Yeah, she still makes them. I'm sure she'd love your help. Should I tell her to call you?"

Her mom paused. "She can call me tomorrow at 11:30 because I'm talking to that lawyer of yours at 11:00."

"Okay, great," Jeff said. "I will let them know." He met Alicia's stunned gaze. "I'll see you later."

"Wait," Alicia said, glancing at her mom, who'd turned back to the fire. "I'll walk you out." She followed Jeff out of the house, and before he could step off the porch, she grabbed his arm.

He turned to face her, his eyebrows raised, as if he was surprised she'd followed him.

"You don't have to do all of this," she said. "I mean, you're going way above and beyond this friendship thing. Even I know that Dawson would never work for free, and does your mom really need help with her jewelry business?"

He grinned.

"Jeff." She moved closer and lowered her voice. "My mom is a really difficult person. I feel bad that you're in the middle of this."

Jeff placed his hands on her shoulders. "I want to help your mom. I want to help you. You're just going to have to live with that."

Alicia exhaled. He was really close, and she strangely felt like either kissing him or crying. So she should probably go back into the house before she did either. "I just don't know if I can ever thank you."

"I'm not looking for thanks," he said. Then he leaned down and kissed her cheek.

Alicia was so startled, she didn't move for a moment. Before she could come up with any sort of response, he said, "See you tomorrow. Call me when you get the police report, and we can conference Dawson in. It would be good to have a strategy before he calls your mom."

He moved away, and Alicia nodded numbly. She remained on the porch as she watched him climb into his SUV and drive away. She might have waved goodbye, or she might have just stared at him blankly. She wasn't entirely sure.

By the time she went back inside, her mom was curled up on the couch under a pile of dusty afghans, sound asleep. Alicia locked the front door and turned off a couple of lights, leaving the living room one on for her mom. Then she changed from her hostess dress and climbed into her bed.

When she closed her eyes, she saw Jeff's blue eyes watching her. She saw him leaning toward her. She felt his lips on her cheek.

No, she told herself. *He's just being a friend.* Nothing more. But her heart wasn't listening to her brain. Her heart was imagining what it might be like to kiss Jeff. To be pulled into his arms, and to have his lips on hers . . .

Alicia burrowed under her covers and wished she could just get this night over with—all of it. From her mom's arrest to the spinning thoughts in her head over Jeff. She couldn't think of him as anything more than a friend. She couldn't survive another heartbreak over him. She still hadn't recovered from the last one.

It was a long time before she fell asleep.

When she awoke to the morning sun, Alicia's first thought was that it was a new day. Her mom was safely at home. Jeff was going to help them.

Alicia checked on her mom, who was still sleeping on the

couch, before she got into the shower. She knew she had to make a phone call to her dad, and although she dreaded it, she hoped that her dad would help her find a solution. The more she thought about her mom wandering in the neighborhood at night, the more worried she became about going to work that night. But if she didn't go to work, or if she quit her job, then she might go crazy herself. Not to mention completely broke.

She dressed, then blow-dried her hair. By the time she came out of her bathroom, her mom was up and eating some scrambled eggs. Alicia knew better than to ask if her mom had made enough for two, so she searched through the pantry for a box of cereal.

She moved aside two herb pots that contained dried dirt and dead plants to make room for her cereal bowl at the table. All the while her mom eyed her, making sure Alicia didn't somehow damage the herb pots.

When her mom apparently deemed the dead herbs safe, she left the kitchen and turned on the TV in the front room. This was a good sign. Her mom hadn't nagged Alicia or tried to start an argument. She also wasn't searching through boxes, frantic to find something. Watching TV usually meant that her mood was mellow.

Alicia's phone dinged. An email had come through from Officer Leo Russo. She thought of the gangly dark-haired kid who'd always been playing pranks in school. He'd grown into a well-built police officer who was all business. She opened the attachment and read through the police report while the TV droned in the next room.

Her mother was being charged with trespassing on private property, petty theft, and obstruction of justice. Alicia scanned the account written up by the arresting officer. It sounded like her mother didn't cooperate much; the officers had asked her plenty of questions, which she'd refused to answer.

Alicia exhaled. She was debating about whether to call her dad before or after her mom talked to Dawson Harris. She hated to keep relying on Jeff, but she had zero experience with this kind of stuff, so she saved the PDF on her phone, then texted it to Jeff. *Call me when you have a chance to look over this.*

When he called her about twenty minutes later, Alicia was in her room, the door locked.

"Thanks for calling," she said, trying not to think about his innocent kiss on her cheek last night.

"How are you?" he asked.

Of course he would ask that. "I slept in."

"That's good," he said. "I think I've given up on ever getting a full night's sleep again."

Alicia sighed. "I'm sorry about that. If I hadn't called—"

"That not it at all. I'm glad you called." He lowered his voice. "I *want* you to call."

Something about the tone of his voice made her already fast pulse quicken.

"I don't know how to thank you for all you've done," Alicia said. "I mean, I'd make you cookies or brownies, but I really don't trust my mom's kitchen. You saw how unsanitary and dangerous it is."

He chuckled.

"What's funny?"

"I don't think a kitchen can be *dangerous*—just maybe a person in it."

"That too," Alicia said. "My mom doesn't like me to move things around. She's pretty territorial."

"Yeah, I can see that."

"About that . . . I'm sorry you had to see the house last night. It's pretty terrible."

"Stop apologizing," Jeff said. "Your mom's ill. You don't have to apologize for that. You've been amazing with her."

Alicia exhaled. "I just don't know what else to do, you know. How do I keep her out of trouble? Lock her in the house? I don't even know if I should go to work tonight."

"We can figure something out," Jeff said. "It's not good for you to be stuck in that house either."

"Yeah, I know." She stood from her bed and crossed to the window to look out at the snowy backyard. "Remember when we used to have wars on the swings? See who could swing higher, and then we'd try to make each other fall off."

Jeff chuckled. "Until that time when I broke my hand. Our parents were so mad, they grounded me for a week."

"You got lucky," Alicia said. "I was grounded for two weeks."

"But you didn't have to wear a cast."

"True." Alicia was smiling, but then she sobered. "That was the summer before my parents split up. It seems like everything sort of changed after that."

"We were both fourteen," Jeff said. "Everyone goes through changes at that age."

Alicia nodded, even though Jeff couldn't see her. The silence between them stretched.

"Hey," Jeff said. "I need to talk to you about something. It's sort of . . . well, it's sort of awkward."

She stiffened. "Okay, what is it?"

"In person," Jeff said. "I'll come over with my mom later, if your mom gives the all-clear on the jewelry thing."

Now Alicia was really curious.

"In the meantime, I texted that police report over to Dawson, and he'll call your mom at 11:00 like she asked." He paused. "It looks like they're throwing everything at her that they can. But that's normal for a police report. A lot can change between now and the court appearance."

"Do you think she'll have to do jail time?" Alicia asked, her heart hammering at the thought.

"No," Jeff said. "I talked to Dawson for a few minutes last night, and even though I didn't know the exact charges, he had a pretty decent idea of them. He said if there are any felony charges, he can get them reduced to misdemeanors."

"Good," Alicia said. "Although I hate everything about this still, I'm glad there's more hope than I thought."

"Can I get your dad's phone number?"

Alicia frowned. "I haven't called him yet to tell him, but I plan to this morning."

"That's good," Jeff said. "I want to give the number to Dawson, because we might need a character statement from your dad."

"They're divorced; how is that going to help?" Alicia asked.

"Both your mom and dad lived in the neighborhood together for years," Jeff said. "Dawson wonders if there were any issues with those neighbors in the past."

"I don't think so," Alicia said. "But I was much more wrapped up in my teenage self than what any neighbor disputes might be."

"Me too."

They both went silent for a moment, Alicia still curious about what he had to tell her in person.

"Oh, it looks like Dawson's calling," Jeff said.

"Talk to you later," Alicia said and hung up.

Before she lost her nerve, she pulled up her contacts and called her dad. He answered on the first ring as if he'd been waiting for her call.

"Dad?" she said.

"Oh, hi, I was about to make a call, and your number came through," he said.

"I'm glad you answered," she said. "I have something to tell you about Mom." For the next ten minutes she explained the situation to her dad about all that Jeff was doing, and about the lawyer phone call that would happen at 11:00.

After uttering a couple of curse words, her dad asked, "The lawyer's helping your mom for free? How's that possible?"

"Jeff said—"

"Are you sure you want to trust Jeff Finch?" her dad cut in. "Last I knew, you guys hadn't even talked to each other since high school, and now suddenly he's very much involved in your life."

Alicia knew her dad meant well, but she had been on her own when it came to dealing with her mom, and Jeff had stepped in to help without a second thought.

"Like I told you, honey," her dad went on. "Your mom's an adult. If she can't take care of herself or stay out of trouble, then she needs to go to that residential facility. She'll have care around the clock, she'll have friends, and she'll do a lot of activities."

"She'll go crazy in a place like that," Alicia said, her skin heating up with indignation. This was where every conversation with her dad went. Stick her mom in an institution somewhere and forget about her.

Her dad wasn't finished. "You've watched too many old movies. The residential facilities are like resorts now. They treat the mentally ill patients like Hollywood VIPs."

"Stop, Dad," Alicia said. "I need to get through whatever these charges are against Mom. Other than this incident, she's been improving."

Her dad scoffed. "Improving? How?"

"Well, I threw away a pair hot pads the other day, and even though we argued about it, she calmed down after," Alicia said. "We actually had a decent conversation about it."

"Over a hot pad?" he said. "Sounds like progress."

Alicia was tempted to hang up on her dad. She didn't know who she was more annoyed with right now—her sane parent, or her insane one.

Sixteen

Jeff pulled into the Waters' driveway with his mom in the passenger seat of his SUV. His mom had done him a favor and called Mrs. Waters at 11:30. It seemed their conversation went better than he expected, and she'd invited Jeff's mom to come over and do a jewelry-making demonstration. So Jeff had picked up his mom, and on the drive over, he'd explained how Alicia and he had become friends again.

True to her nature, his mom was able to get more than the basic story out of him. He confessed more to her than he did to himself. Now, that they'd arrived, he turned off the engine.

"I hope you know what you're doing," his mom said.

He looked over at her. His mom was always well put together, with her salon-styled-and-dyed hair. Her careful makeup. Like usual, her outfit coordinated with her earrings and necklace. He supposed it was part of the reason she was so successful with her Etsy shop. She frequently got compliments on her jewelry, then handed out her business card.

"I don't think I've ever known what I'm doing when it comes to Alicia," Jeff said. "I feel like a bumbling teenager when I'm around her."

His mom patted his arm. "If she's as beautiful and sweet as she used to be, I don't blame you. I could never figure out why you just didn't apologize back in high school and get on with it."

"She hated me," Jeff said simply.

"And now?" His mom's eyes were mischievous.

"She doesn't hate me."

"Well," his mom said. "I'm looking forward to seeing the woman who you've spent ten years trying to get over. And heaven knows, it's been years since I've seen Lila. If she's as changed as you say she is, we might not have much in common anymore."

"Just be yourself," Jeff said. "Everyone who knows you loves you."

His mom popped open her door. "Let's hope you're right, because if Alicia is as loyal to her mom as you say she is, we've got to win over Lila Waters to convince Alicia to give you another chance."

"Don't say that, Mom," Jeff said with a groan. Why had he confessed anything to his mother? If he really thought about it, his mom had guessed most of it anyway. He hadn't ever stopped thinking about Alicia. He hadn't ever moved on. And even in high school, he knew she was the girl he never wanted to lose. He'd just been too much of an idiot to stand up for what he knew then.

His mom pushed her door open and climbed out of the SUV, flashing a smile in his direction before she marched up to the house.

Jeff grabbed her jewelry kit from the back seat, then

caught up with her just as she rang the doorbell. When Mrs. Waters answered the door, Jeff was more than surprised. The woman was dressed in normal clothes, and it looked as if she'd showered and brushed her hair.

"Hello, Beth," Mrs. Waters said, her voice tentative but friendly.

Another surprise.

"Hi, Lila," his mom said. "It's great to see you. I can't believe how long it's been since I've been back home."

Mrs. Waters raised her brows.

"I've always thought of this neighborhood as home," his mom continued. "Do you color your hair, or are you just naturally still dark?"

Mrs. Waters touched her hair. It was dark like Alicia's, but there were definitely plenty of silver strands through it. "This is natural."

"It looks great," his mom said. "I've become a slave to the salon. I don't recommend it. Once you start, you can't stop."

"That's what I've heard," Mrs. Waters said, her voice gaining strength. "Come inside. I have the table ready for you." Her gaze cut to Jeff as if she was noticing him for the first time.

"I hope you don't mind that I brought Jeff with me," his mom said. "He's my driver because my car's in the shop."

It was the truth, but his mom could have easily driven his dad's car.

Mrs. Waters didn't say anything, but she did open the door wider, so Jeff took that as an invitation. He followed his mother inside. Everything looked the same as it did yesterday, and he wondered what his mom was thinking as they walked through the living room to the kitchen.

The kitchen table had a crate full of picture frames at one

end, but the rest of the table was clear. And by comparing the table to the counters full of junk, Jeff knew it was a feat to have this table so clean.

"Oh my goodness," his mom said. "Are you saving those picture frames for anything?"

"I . . . I just like to hold onto them," Mrs. Waters said, her eyes narrowing.

"They're always looking for old picture frames at the assisted living center," his mom gushed. "They paint them, then put dried flowers behind the glass. If you want to ever get rid of them, I'll take them off your hands."

Mrs. Waters blinked. "I'll let you know."

"Great," his mom said. "Jeff, set that jewelry case right here. Then make yourself scarce. I don't want any distractions."

Mrs. Waters looked at him directly. "You can watch TV if you want. I don't know what Alicia is doing. She's always up to something."

Before Mrs. Waters could say something else negative about her daughter, Jeff went out into the living room. He nearly ran into Alicia. He grabbed her arms, mostly to steady himself.

"There you are," he said, looking down at her. She smelled like lemon and strawberries. Good enough to taste. He tried to shake that thought away. But it didn't help that she was wearing a light pink lipstick, which only brought more attention to her mouth.

She smiled, and he realized her hazel eyes were almost green today.

"Here I am," she said. "It sounds like our moms are getting along just fine."

"They are," Jeff said, realizing he was still holding onto her arms. He dropped his hands and shoved them into his pockets. They both listened for a moment. His mom laughed, Mrs. Waters said something, and his mom laughed again.

Jeff smiled back at Alicia. "This is good, right?"

"Very good," she said. "Who would have thought?"

They listened again to their moms chatting away. His mom had a heart of gold, that was for sure. But then again, Mrs. Waters acted differently around his mom. Maybe a friend would help out Mrs. Waters.

"How did the phone call go with Dawson and your mom?" he asked Alicia.

She put a hand to her lips, then motioned for him to follow her. She led him down the hall a little way and stopped where there was an opening to the boxes. "It went well," Alicia said. "My mom's still defending her actions, though. My mom had written down Dawson's phone number, so I called him a little bit later. He seems to think that she'll just have to pay a fine for trespassing and get the obstruction of justice and petty theft dropped. He also said the money we paid for bail will be subtracted from the fine."

"Good." He liked being alone with her, even though it was in a hallway full of boxes and he could still hear the murmur of their moms' voices from here.

"Oh, that reminds me," Alicia continued, touching his arm. "I haven't been able to get that money I owe you yet."

"It's all right," Jeff said, looking down at her hand on his arm. "Even if you completely forgot and never paid me back, no worries."

"You can't do that," Alicia said, dropping her hand and gazing back up at him.

He found himself leaning toward her, and she wasn't backing away. "Do what?"

"Be so nice. I mean, every day I feel like I owe you more and more."

"Don't feel that way," Jeff said. "I mean, I don't want you to think that anything I do for you is because I expect something in return."

She bit her lip. "What is it that you wanted to talk to me about in person?"

Jeff exhaled and rubbed the back of his neck. He wanted to be completely honest with Alicia, but he didn't know he'd feel this nervous. "I need to tell you something, but I don't want to freak you out. Nothing has to change between us. Things can stay the same . . . if you want."

"What is it?" she said, frown lines appearing between her eyebrows.

Jeff held her gaze. He had to tell her, and he had to tell her now. For better or for worse. "I've spent the past ten years chasing after a ghost. Dating women who never matched up to you. Thinking that I could forget you."

Her eyes widened, and she opened her mouth to say something. He put a finger to her lips to stop her. "Let me say this."

She nodded.

He lowered his finger, then he traced the edge of her jaw with his fingers. She didn't move, but she didn't pull away either. He dropped his hand. "I know I told you I'm sorry for being an idiot at our prom. But what I didn't tell you is that I had a crush on you, too. For years. I'm not sure when it started—probably when we were ten."

She inhaled sharply and just stared at him.

"And . . ." He started. "It turns out that I still have a crush on you."

She just stared at him like she didn't believe him. But he'd confessed it all. He'd told her the absolute truth. Why wasn't she saying anything? "Say something."

Her lips quirked. Was she going to laugh at him? Treat this all as a joke?

"Anything," he prompted.

"Anything," she repeated, and stepped toward him.

They were nearly touching now. Jeff could smell her strawberry scent; he could hear her breathing. When she placed her hands on his shoulders, he leaned toward her until they were sharing the same breathing space. "Alicia—"

"Just kiss me, Jeff," she whispered, closing her eyes.

His heart tripped. Cradling her face, he pressed his mouth against her warm lips. Her hands moved behind his neck as she kissed him back, and all he could think of was that she tasted like lemons and strawberries and every good memory in his life. She pressed closer, and he moved his hands over her shoulders, down her back, and then tugged her hips against him.

Every inch of her fit every inch of him like a perfect puzzle. He couldn't believe he was kissing her, and he didn't know if he'd be able to stop now that they'd started.

Their kissing turned more frantic, more passionate. Then Alicia broke off and tugged his arm to lead him down the hall. She opened a door and pulled him inside, then shut the door, drawing him to her again. He assumed they were in her bedroom, but they were kissing again before he had a chance to look around.

Jeff backed her up against the door, and she clung to him as he explored her mouth, her jawline, her neck. He didn't want to stop, but he knew he should. Their moms were in the kitchen, and he didn't want Alicia to think he was after only one thing. Because with her, it was different, everything was different. He didn't ever want to hurt her again.

He lifted his head and forced himself to catch his breath. "Does this mean you have a crush on me, too?"

Her eyes were bright when their gazes met, and her cheeks flushed pink. Jeff had never seen her look so beautiful.

She smiled. "Maybe."

He groaned. "You're killing me."

Alicia laughed. She raised up on her tiptoes and pressed her pink lips against his, then pulled away much too soon. She ran her hands down his chest, then wrapped her arms about his waist and laid her head against his shoulder.

He wrapped his arms about her and buried his face in her hair. He inhaled, and just breathed her in for a moment, not thinking about anything beyond right now, right here. He felt like he'd waited a lifetime to kiss Alicia, and now that he had, he regretted all of the wasted years of silence. Why did he think he could find a woman to replace Alicia?

His phone started to ring, and he groaned.

"You can answer that," Alicia said.

"I don't want to."

"What if it's Dawson?" she asked.

Jeff sighed and lifted his head, then reached for his phone. "It's Dawson." He answered the call, keeping one arm about Alicia's waist. He wasn't ready to let her go.

"I've got a court date set up in two weeks," Dawson said on the other end of the line.

"So soon?" Jeff said.

"Pine Valley isn't exactly hopping with misdemeanor cases," Dawson said. "Is Alicia with you? I've been trying to call her. I didn't know when I can call her mom—it seems I need an appointment just to call her."

"Yeah, she's with me," Jeff said. "You can talk to her." He pulled the phone from his ear. "Dawson wants to talk to you. He says he hasn't been able to reach you."

"My phone's in the living room." Alicia took the phone and answered.

As she talked to Dawson, Jeff wrapped his arms around her from behind and rested his chin on her shoulder. He could hear most of what Dawson said, so when Alicia hung up, she turned around to face him. "Do you think my mom will be ready that soon?"

"Like Dawson said, if he and the prosecutor can agree to terms in advance of meeting with the judge, the court appearance will just be a formality." He liked the relief he saw in her eyes.

"That would be great," Alicia said. "Now I just need to figure out how to keep her out of trouble."

"Jeff?" his mom's voice came from somewhere outside the bedroom.

Alicia smiled. "I think we've been busted."

He put a finger to his lips, then opened the door. He stepped through and walked down the hallway to find his mom in the living room with Mrs. Waters. They were sorting through a stack of CDs. "The residents will love these," his mom said. Then she saw him.

"Oh, there you are," his mom said in a completely innocent voice. "Lila is letting us take the picture frames off her hands. Can you load them in your SUV and drop them off at the assisted living center on your way to work? Lila told me that Alicia can take me home later."

Jeff's mouth nearly fell open. From everything he'd seen and heard, Mrs. Waters never got rid of anything. "Sure, I can do that." He glanced behind him to see Alicia. She looked as surprised as he felt.

He grabbed the crate off the table in the kitchen. And while he loaded the crate into the back seat of the SUV, he wondered if this was a step in the right direction. Or would Mrs. Waters regret her decisions to give away the old picture frames? He hurried back into the house only to be met by Alicia with a box of CDs.

He took the box from her. "What's going on?" Jeff said as they walked to the SUV together.

Alicia rubbed her arms against the cold air. "I don't know, but I'm so glad your mom came over. I can't believe my mom wants to give this stuff away. It's a miracle."

Jeff set the box in the back seat, then turned and pulled her into his arms.

She came willingly, but whispered, "What's happening between us, Jeff?"

He drew away to look at her. "I was hoping I could take you out on a date. You know, be more than friends."

Alicia smiled, but there were a lot of questions behind that smile. "I'll have to check my schedule."

"Do that, then let me know." He pressed a light kiss on her mouth, wanting to convince her that this was the beginning of something real. He was no longer the same man he'd been. "The sooner the better, except right now I've got to meet a client at a house."

"Go," Alicia said, playfully pushing him away. "You've achieved your hero quota for the day."

Jeff laughed and climbed into the SUV. He'd have just enough time to drop off the boxes at the assisted living center. Yet, all he wanted to do was go back into that house and keep hanging out with Alicia. He wanted to find a way to gain her full trust, because he planned on their relationship only growing stronger.

Seventeen

He's too good to be true, Alicia thought as she watched Jeff's SUV pull away until it turned the corner. Yes, they were friends now. She'd completely forgiven him. But she wasn't sure she was entirely convinced of his commitment to her.

He'd just broken up with a gorgeous woman and was likely on the rebound. Besides, what about all his pictures on social media? It was obvious he enjoyed the fast-paced lifestyle. And everything between them was shiny and new . . . like a honeymoon period. They'd just renewed their friendship, and with so many memories between them, they couldn't help but still be bonded.

Yet, Alicia stayed in the driveway, lost in her own thoughts as she remembered the way he'd kissed her . . . after she'd practically demanded that he do so. Okay, so she had a moment of weakness, well, a lot of moments. When it came to Jeff, she supposed that she'd always loved him. As a friend, of course. She knew she was in real danger of falling in love with him. But could she ever truly trust him? Was she about to be another woman he had a relationship with, then move on, leaving her broken hearted?

Perhaps he'd taken this apology thing too far, and he'd mixed up having a crush on her with feeling relieved that he'd been able to make good on his promise to make up his past mistakes.

Alicia turned toward the house and walked to the porch. The cold air was good for her—it kept her mind more clear and senses alert. With a sinking feeling, she knew she should probably turn Jeff down for a date. He was on the rebound. Their worlds were miles apart. Despite how helpful he'd been, he couldn't possibly want to deal with her mess of a life on a daily basis.

When she entered the house, a new determination about her, she was pleased to see that her mom and Jeff's mom, Beth, were sitting at the table and chatting while they pieced together earrings.

"That took a while," her mom said when Alicia came in. "Beth says that we should go out to eat for dinner at your restaurant tonight."

Alicia swallowed. She was stunned and wasn't sure what to say. "I—I could call to see if I can get you a table." She wasn't quite envisioning her mom going out to dinner at such a fancy place.

"That would be wonderful," Beth said in a bright voice. "Jeff said you got him a table the other night."

Alicia gave a weak smile, then moved past them. "I'll call work and let you know." She went into her bedroom and shut the door, exhaling. Her mind was spinning, her heart thumping, and she was trying to comprehend all these sudden changes in her life. She knew one thing, and that was that Beth was good for her mom. Alicia called the restaurant and was able to get a table for two. That accomplished, she got ready for work.

When she came out of her room wearing one of her hostess dresses, she asked her mom, "Do you have a way to get to the restaurant?"

"My husband will pick us up; then we'll get my car," Beth said. "It's ready at the shop."

Alicia hesitated, glancing at her mom, wondering if all of this was truly going to work out.

"Go on," her mom said, perfectly conciliatory. "You don't want to be late."

Alicia smiled, though she still felt unsure. What if her mom had an anxiety attack? How would Beth deal with it?

"We'll see you in a couple of hours," Beth said with a nod. "I'm looking forward to testing out the place. I haven't been there since the new owner took over."

When Alicia left the house, her mom was describing some of the leftovers Alicia had brought home. She climbed in her car and drove to the restaurant, hoping her mom's friendship with Beth would be a good thing and that the court date would cement into her mom's mind that she couldn't get into the neighbor's trash anymore.

Once at work, Alicia greeted Gwen, who seemed extra cheerful.

"You've got a permanent grin on your face," Alicia said as they straightened chairs about the restaurant.

Gwen shrugged, but kept smiling.

"What's going on?" Alicia said, putting her hands on her hips. "Does it have something to do with Seth?"

Gwen eyes widened. Then she looked over her shoulder. When she looked at Alicia again, she said, "If you say anything to anyone else, I'll kill you."

Alicia laughed. "All right, you have my word."

"We went out to lunch today," Gwen said, her blush softening to a pink.

"And?"

"And . . . it was nice. He's not what I expected." Gwen moved past Alicia and straightened a set of salt and pepper shakers on the next table over. "I don't want to say too much— or you know, karma."

Alicia raised her brows, unsure of exactly what Gwen meant. But the front door had opened. It was only 5:30, but some people came early for their reservation. "You secret is safe," Alicia said, then headed to the hostess stand. She almost tripped when she saw the woman waiting there—Paige. Alicia didn't know her last name, but by the harsh look on the woman's face, Alicia guessed she hadn't come to eat in the restaurant.

The woman was wearing a fitted white sheath dress, and her bare arms were draped in gold bracelets. Her stilettos were a nude color, which only made her legs look like a Victoria Secret supermodel. Who dressed like that when there was snow on the ground?

"Can I help you?" Alicia asked. Maybe the woman had forgotten something last week when she'd come with Jeff? A purse? A jacket?

"It *is* you," Paige said in a low voice as if she didn't want to be overheard by the waiters in the open restaurant area.

Alicia lifted her chin. "Do I know you?" She was playing dumb, but she didn't know how else to handle the sudden appearance of Jeff's ex-girlfriend.

"You know perfectly well who I am," Paige continued. "Jeff couldn't keep his eyes off you, and when I realized that your name was 'Alicia,' I eventually put two and two together."

"I'm not sure what you're talking about," Alicia said, resting her hands on the hostess stand and gripping the edges.

Paige scoffed. She placed her own hands on the other side of the hostess stand and leaned forward. "The first night I met him, we both got pretty wasted. He told me all about his best friend in high school, how you had a crush on him, and how he ditched you at Prom. He laughed, but I could tell that he was still beating himself up over it. So I took pity on him."

"I don't really want to know—"

But the woman kept talking, her eyes bulging as she stared down Alicia. "We went back to my place, and we've been dating ever since. For *three months*. Until last week when we ran into you, *here*, of all places. Next thing I know, he's trying to break up with me."

Alicia held up her hand. "I didn't break you guys up. Until you came into the restaurant, I hadn't seen Jeff in ten years."

"Ah-ha," Paige said, pointing a blood-red nail at Alicia. "So you admit it."

"I'm not admitting anything," Alicia said. "I don't know why you're here, but maybe you should take all of this crazy talk to Jeff."

"Crazy? *Me?*" Paige's voice was no longer low and controlled.

Alicia was glad there were no actual customers in the restaurant.

"You're an evil woman, Alicia whatever-your-name-is," Paige spat out. "But you've made a big mistake messing with me. Did you know we were together only two nights ago? He couldn't keep his hands off me."

Alicia's stomach turned over.

A movement to Alicia's right caught her eye. Gwen had arrived.

"I think you'd better leave, ma'am," Gwen said, folding her arms. Even though she was shorter than Paige, Gwen had a fierce expression on her face.

"Oh, you bet I'm leaving," Paige said. "I just wanted proof, and I got it." She held up her cell phone and snapped a picture of Alicia. Then she turned and walked out of the restaurant before Alicia or Gwen could react.

When the door swung shut behind Paige, Alicia exhaled. "Well."

"Is that all you can say?" Gwen asked, grasping Alicia's shoulders and turning her to face her. "Are *you* all right? That woman had crazy eyes. Who was she?"

"Jeff's ex-girlfriend," Alicia said. But if they'd been together only a couple of nights ago, maybe she wasn't an ex.

"Ohhh . . ." Gwen raised her brows.

"I think she is a little crazy," Alicia said. *And I'm going a little crazy thinking of the two of them together.* "She's blaming me for their breakup."

"Well, what do you think?" Gwen said. "I mean, it is quite a coincidence."

"No," Alicia said, feeling her face flush. "At least, I don't think so."

"Something happened between the two of you, didn't it?" Gwen said, holding her gaze. "Did you kiss him?"

Alicia stepped back and raised her hands to her cheeks. "Is it that obvious?"

Gwen smirked. "Only to me because I'm your friend. I can't believe it! I need details."

"Um, no. It was a mistake." Alicia nodded toward the door. "Paige made it clear that things aren't over between them."

Gwen put her hands on her hips. "You're totally avoiding my question."

Alicia gave Gwen a small smile. "There's a lot of history between Jeff and me, that's all. And I'm not really interested in a fling."

The door opened, effectively cutting off their conversation. A couple walked in, early for their reservation. Alicia welcomed them, her mind still going over what Paige had said to her. It seemed that even though Jeff had said they were broken up, he was still seeing her. Alicia was so confused. If what Paige said was true, then Jeff was the worst kind of player. And what was Paige going to use the picture for? She should let Jeff know, but Alicia already felt like she'd brought enough drama and problems to Jeff's life. Besides, she didn't want anything to do with him if he was on the rebound. Clearly, he couldn't stay away from Paige.

Alicia tried to forget about Paige, and Jeff too, as she went through the motions of her job. The only bright spot was when her mom and Lila showed up for their dinner reservation. Her mom had pulled her hair back into a twist, secured with a hairclip, and she wore a dress that Alicia hadn't seen in years. The navy floral dress was boxy on her mom's thin frame, but Alicia thought she still looked amazing.

The two women sat at table four, and that gave Alicia a view of them while they ate. She felt like crying every time she got a glimpse of them talking, laughing, and having a good time. No matter what happened between her and Jeff, Alicia owed him her deepest gratitude.

A couple of texts came through from Jeff during her shift, but she ignored them both.

She needed some time to think through her feelings. If only they hadn't kissed, this would all be easier. She wouldn't have the memory of kissing him, and how her every nerve had been aware of him while she was in his arms.

But by the time she drove home, she hadn't arrived at any brilliant answers. She only knew that she had to turn off whatever feelings she had for Jeff Finch.

Eighteen

Jeff stared at the image of Alicia on his phone, the image Paige had texted over that night. *Your old girlfriend admitted to cheating with you*, Paige had texted.

Jeff knew instantly Paige had been lying, but what was true was that Paige somehow snapped this picture of Alicia. And by the background and what Alicia was wearing, it was obviously at the restaurant.

Abandoning the sandwich he'd bought at a drive-through on the way home from work, he walked to the back of his house where the sliding glass doors opened up to a large deck, and beyond that a view of the ski resort. He stared into the darkness, wondering how he'd gotten himself into this situation. Before calling Paige to confront her, he called Dawson.

When Dawson answered the phone, he said, "Who's in jail now?"

"No one that I know," Jeff said. "But I wouldn't mind getting a restraining order on my ex-girlfriend."

"Paige?" Dawson asked. "Are you serious?"

"Mostly serious," Jeff said. "She's harassing Alicia and who knows what else. I thought I'd call Paige and give her some legal mumbo jumbo that would be intimidating enough for her to chill."

Dawson scoffed. "A scorned woman is a dangerous woman."

Jeff's heart thumped. "What are you saying?"

"I'm saying that a restraining order might not be such a bad idea."

Jeff exhaled. "I don't really want it to go that far."

"Yeah, I get that," Dawson said. "Hopefully just bringing it up will have a strong enough effect."

"I hope so too," Jeff said. When he hung up with Dawson a few minutes later, Jeff scrolled through his texts. Alicia hadn't replied to his earlier messages, and now with the picture sent from Paige, he understood why.

With a groan, he pulled up his contacts and called Paige. She answered on the first ring.

"Hi, baby," she said.

Anger shot through him, not only at the sickly sweet tone of her voice, but at the endearment she chose to call him. "When did you talk to Alicia?" he asked, although he could guess.

"Oooh, someone's grumpy," she said, as if she didn't know how to answer a simple question. "I have a cure for that. Want me to come over?"

Jeff wondered how in the world he'd ever thought he wanted to date Paige. Had he totally lost his mind? "Look, Paige, tell me what happened."

"I just told her the truth," Paige said, her tone a little less sweet now. "Why don't you ask her since she's your girlfriend now?"

"She's not . . . Our relationship isn't any of your business. You and I broke up, remember Paige?"

"Whatever, Jeff," Paige said. "Men like you always come back."

"I'm not coming back," he said. "And if you bother Alicia again, I'm going to file for a restraining order."

Paige went silent for a moment. "You wouldn't dare."

"I've already talked to Dawson about it," he said. "Don't push me."

She scoffed. "Don't push *you*? You're the cheater, and a liar. I should get a restraining order for *you*."

"I'm not the one who's confronting your old boyfriends and texting you pictures," Jeff said, using all of his willpower not to yell at her.

"Stop trying to make yourself look better than me," she retorted. "Alicia knows the truth about you now. If she decides to put up with you, then you both deserve each other."

"Look," he said. "Can we just part ways and not mess with each other's lives?" His answer was a click on the other end of the line. Paige had hung up on him. Jeff didn't know whether that was a good thing or bad thing.

He leaned his head against the cold glass sliding door and scrolled through his latest texts. Alicia had never texted him back, and she should be off work by now. He called her number, but there was no answer. Frustrated, he exhaled. Maybe he'd moved too fast with Alicia. He'd confessed his feelings too soon. The kissing had scared her off. He hoped that was all, and that whatever Paige had told Alicia, she hadn't believed it.

He opened the sliding door and flipped on the switch for the hot tub. Then he removed the cover, and went to his bedroom to change into a pair of board shorts. He hoped that the hot water would help him sleep tonight. With all the lights off, he'd have a clear view of the snow on the mountains beneath the moonlight.

As the water bubbled around him, and the steam heated his face, he closed his eyes. He was half-asleep in the hot tub when his phone rang. His eyes popped open, and he looked to the deck chair where he'd left his phone. From his position, he could see it was Alicia. So he scrambled out of the hot tub, dripping wet. The cold hit him with full force.

"Hello?" he answered in a breathless voice.

"Jeff?" Alicia's voice sounded strange.

"Is everything okay?" He grabbed the towel and awkwardly wrapped it around his waist.

"Yeah, I mean, I think so," she said. "I didn't know if you'd be awake."

"I was just in the hot tub," he said. "Hoping that I'll be able to sleep better after."

When she didn't respond, he said, "I'm alone, if that's what you were wondering."

"Oh, I wasn't."

Jeff had heard the doubt in her voice though. He exhaled as he walked into the kitchen and perched on one of the stools. "So . . . I talked to Paige. I told her to stop bothering you. I don't know what's gotten into her."

"Did she tell you what she said at the restaurant?" Alicia asked.

"Her version, which I don't totally believe."

"I don't believe everything she told me either," Alicia said. "But there must be some truth in it, especially about the definition of the relationship between the two of you."

"We broke up, you know that," Jeff said. "She might still think we're going to get back together, but that's not true on my end."

"She was pretty convincing, Jeff," Alicia said in a quiet voice. "But that doesn't matter one way or another. I wanted to wait to call you until I knew the best way to say this."

Jeff closed his eyes, waiting for the daggers to be thrown.

"I think you're on the rebound, and as you know, things in my life are very complicated."

She'd said it, and Jeff didn't like it.

"You know I care for you," she continued. "And I'll probably always have a crush on you—although I'm not sure if it's still on the high school Jeff, or the current Jeff."

Okay, that one hurt. "Wait," he interrupted. "I can guess where you're going with this, and I need to say something before you shred me." When she didn't say anything, he continued, "I'm not on the rebound from Paige. I was never in love with her or anything. I had decided to break things off before I even saw you in the restaurant. The fact that I did see you that night was just another confirmation. And if you don't have a crush on the current Jeff, I can live with that. You can even turn me down for the date I asked you on. Our moms can stay friends. I can randomly run into you. Maybe down the road you'll change your mind, and at that point we can reassess and—"

"Jeff," she cut in. "That will still keep the relationship alive. I can't tell my mom not to work with your mom. I'm glad they're starting to be friends again. But, I just can't . . . be around you. Believe me, I've been thinking about this all night. I have trust issues, and I just need to be with someone I trust— someday—when my mom doesn't need me so much."

The distress in her voice was real, and it tore at Jeff. He wanted to assure her that he could find solutions for her mom; he wanted to beg her to change her mind, to agree to be casual friends. But after kissing her, Jeff knew they could never be casual. And she knew it too.

He rubbed the water droplets from his face with his towel. "So, this is it?"

"I'm sorry," she said in a quiet voice.

"Me too," he said. He didn't know who he was more angry at. Paige or himself. Paige for butting into their lives at such a precarious time. Or himself, for not finding Alicia sooner and giving her the apology she deserved. This was what he deserved, he guessed, for waiting ten years. It turned out that it was too late after all.

"Okay, Alicia, I hear you," Jeff said. "And I get it. I really do. I just want you to know that I haven't changed my mind about you."

He thought he heard her sniffle, but he wasn't sure, because she said a very soft "goodbye" and hung up on him.

Strike two.

Nineteen

Alicia didn't know why she had even thought Jeff might show up at her mom's court date. Of course he wouldn't. Alicia had not only rejected him, but she'd told him she didn't even want to be friends. It had been almost two weeks since their final conversation on the phone, and she'd felt terrible ever since.

But she decided to keep her focus on her mom. She was improving, and in large part, that was due to Beth Finch. The woman had come over regularly, working on jewelry with her mom. They'd even gone to Beth's a few times.

That didn't soften the disappointment Alicia felt in not seeing Jeff come into the courthouse with his mom. Beth had come to offer support and sat on the other side of Alicia's mom on the bench. Dawson sat on the front row, waiting for the clerk to call Alicia's mom's case number. Dawson had been nothing but kind and professional to both Alicia and her mom, and Alicia had found herself more and more impressed with him.

Her mom had even told Alicia she wouldn't mind a smart lawyer as a son-in-law. Alicia had answered back that she was too busy to date right now. Besides, she didn't want to settle in Pine Valley with the possibility of seeing Jeff at any moment. Not that she had seen him for two weeks, though. She often wondered if he was going out of his way to avoid her. Or at least to never eat at Alpine Lodge with any clients or someone he might have started dating.

At least Paige had gone completely silent.

"Lila Waters," the clerk called out.

Dawson stood. "I'm representing Mrs. Waters today." Then he turned and motioned for Alicia's mom to approach the bench.

Watching her mom walk to the front of the courtroom made Alicia feel like she wanted to run after her, to stop the questioning. Mrs. Finch reached over and grasped Alicia's hand. She clung to it thankfully.

Everything happened so fast that Alicia couldn't believe that with just a short conversation, the judge pronounced a fine and called for the next case.

"It's over?" Alicia whispered. "And she only got a fine?"

"Yep," Mrs. Finch said with a smile.

Relief shot through Alicia, and she suddenly felt as light as air. Her mother was walking toward them, Dawson right behind her. He motioned for all of them to step in the hall. Then he spoke quietly to the group. "The bail money will count against the fine, and you can either make payments on the remaining balance or pay in full," he said, looking directly at Alicia's mom. "You're on probation for six months, which means that if you commit another violation, the misdemeanors could become felonies with a second offence. Your fine will double, and you'll be facing jail time."

Her mom's mouth fell open. Then she shut it and swallowed. "All right. I'll just stay home."

Dawson smiled. "Don't stay home, just do what you know is right. You have a great daughter, great friends, and they'll help you stay on track."

Her mom nodded. "Thank you, sir."

"You are most welcome." He flashed his brilliant smile and shook everyone's hands. "Now, I have another client I need to meet with in a few minutes. But don't hesitate to call me with any questions."

Dawson left the group, and Beth stepped forward to hug both of them. "We should go celebrate!" she said. "After you work things out with the finance clerk, of course."

Alicia's mom said, "All right."

"Great," Alicia added, although she was surprised at her mom's quick acceptance. She was holding up a lot better than expected.

After her mom set up a payment plan with the financial clerk, they went outside and decided to take Mrs. Finch's car to the Main Street Café. It was only 11:00 a.m., so the place wasn't crowded, and they got a table quickly. They all selected soup and sandwiches, and Alicia relaxed as her mom and Beth chattered away. Even though their house was still piled with stuff, her mom had been giving more and more away, prodded by Beth. It seemed that the assisted living center had been a welcoming recipient. Although, Alicia suspected that some of the stuff Beth just threw away.

"You should invite him to Pine Valley, then," Beth was saying.

Alicia tuned back into the conversation.

"I don't know if I'm ready yet," her mom said.

"Ready for what?" Alicia asked.

Both women went silent. Then finally her mom said, "Beth thinks I need to have a face-to-face conversation with your father." She swallowed. "We left a lot of things unsaid in the divorce. I haven't spoken to him directly since the day the papers were signed."

Alicia stared at her mom. "Do you . . . think it will help?"

Her mom shrugged. "Beth said that one of her friends started picking at her skin after her divorce. It got so bad, she had to go to the hospital. I think that's why I've been having a hard time getting rid of stuff."

Alicia could only nod. This was what her mom's therapist had said more than once. But apparently with Beth's story about her friend, it was starting to make sense to her mom.

"I'm nervous to see your dad in person," her mom continued. "But with court over, and knowing I only have to pay a fine, I feel like I could maybe have that talk with him."

Alicia exhaled. She was literally speechless.

"We can be in the same room if you need us to be," Beth said, resting her hand on Lila's shoulder.

"Thanks," her mom said. "I'll let you know. Once I call him." She gave a nervous laugh.

"Mom?" a deep voice said from the direction of the front of the café.

Alicia looked over, knowing before she even saw him that it was Jeff.

"Jeff!" Beth said. "I didn't know you were coming here."

Jeff's eyes locked on Alicia, their blue color brighter since his pale blue dress shirt only accented his eyes. Despite the cold weather, he wasn't wearing a coat, and she couldn't help but remember how his arms had held her when they kissed. His dark hair was tousled, likely from the wind outside. It was then that Alicia realized they were only about a block from his office, so he'd probably walked over here.

"Hi," Jeff said to Alicia, then looked at her mom. "How did everything go today?"

He remembered, Alicia thought. *Of course he did.* Beth would have said something.

"It went really great," her mom said in a surprisingly conciliatory tone, especially for talking to Jeff. "Your lawyer friend is very good at what he does."

Jeff nodded. "I'm glad it went well." His gaze flickered to Alicia's, then focused on his mom.

"Why don't you join us for lunch?" Beth said. "We barely ordered."

"I'm grabbing some sandwiches to-go for the office," Jeff said. "Clara and I are working on a couple of contracts."

"Clara's such a dear," his mom said. "How is she doing?"

Alicia's neck felt hot. She knew Clara was Jeff's assistant, but why was she feeling so weird with Beth asking Jeff about her?

"She's great," Jeff said. "I should probably give her a raise. She's really picked up the slack for me recently. Well, I should order." He moved past them and ordered at the counter.

Alicia tried to keep her gaze from straying as he placed his order.

Beth was keeping an eye on him too. "Come and sit while you wait," she said, pulling out the fourth chair at their table.

"Okay," Jeff said and sat down.

This put him right next to Alicia, so close that she could smell the cold air and a hint of spice coming from him. Even though it wasn't yet noon, she noticed the dark stubble on his face as if he hadn't had time to shave this morning.

She tried to focus on what their moms were talking about—something to do with the jewelry company and a late order. But Alicia couldn't focus at all. She was only aware of Jeff sitting next to her, the hard set of his jaw, and the way his elbows were resting inches away on the table. She knew he was as aware of her as she was of him. He was trying not to talk to her, or look at her either.

She wondered if he'd gotten back together with Paige, or maybe he was dating someone else by now. A man like him could never be invisible to the female population.

"You two should come with us," Beth said.

Alicia blinked. She wasn't sure what Beth was talking about.

"I've got several showings this weekend," Jeff said.

"I'm not surprised," Beth said. "The market seems to be on the rise."

"Yeah, it is."

Just then, his order was called, and he rose to collect it. He stopped by the table again on his way out. "Nice to see you, everyone. Have a good day."

The cold air that rushed into the café as he opened the door and left seemed to pierce Alicia.

A young woman came over with their order, and the next few minutes were taken up with arranging sandwiches and soup bowls. Alicia found that she wasn't as hungry as she thought. She took a bite of her melted turkey sandwich, then put it down. Instead, she took a sip of her water.

"You know you should give him a chance," her mom said.

Alicia nearly spit her water out. "What?"

Her mom shrugged. "Beth and I were talking about the two of you. Jeff told her a few things that made sense. Did you know he's never been in a relationship for more than a couple of months?"

Alicia shrugged back. What did that have to do with her?

"And I told Beth it was the same with you," her mom continued. "I shouldn't have been so rude to him when he tried to be friends again. I mean, high school was a long time ago."

Alicia stared at her mom. Where was this attitude two weeks ago?

"I don't have all the answers, Alicia," her mom said. "And heaven knows, I'm not even close to being put together. But now I believe I can be stronger and have a better life."

"That's great, Mom," she said in a faint voice.

Beth smiled. "What your mom is trying to say is that it's time you followed your own desires, Alicia. Don't let the things your parents might be going through stop you from living for yourself."

"Jeff is a nice guy, and you've been friends forever," her mom said, glancing over at Beth. "We won't stand in your way."

Beth laughed. "Definitely not. I'm tired of watching him moon over you."

Alicia groaned and buried her face in her hands. She didn't know whether to laugh or cry.

"She's got it too," Beth said to Alicia's mom. "Maybe we should set them up. That would be funny, don't you think?"

Alicia was done. She rose to her feet. "I've got some errands to run, and then I'm meeting Gwen later."

"Let us drive you back to the courthouse," Beth said.

"It's okay. I can walk," Alicia said. "I have a stop to make on the way."

Beth smiled. "All right, dear. We'll see you later."

Alicia could only nod, because she had too many emotions at the surface. She left the café and welcomed the cold wind on her face as she walked to the courthouse to get her car. It was ironic she felt more miserable now that her mother was actually improving. Alicia was also mad that her mom had changed her mind about Jeff.

Alicia felt like a yo-yo. By the time she reached her car, a few tears had fallen. But she'd swallowed most of them back. She could stay strong, and she could be happy for her mom's improvement. It might even mean she'd be free to move away from Pine Valley again.

She'd miss her job, of course, and she's miss Gwen. She'd even miss the pleasant person her mom was becoming. But she'd already made her decision about Jeff, so he shouldn't be a person she'd miss.

Twenty

"Thank you, sir," Jeff said, shaking the buyer's hand who'd just bought his Lamborghini. Jeff was sad to see it go, but it was a weight off as well. He didn't have to worry about making sure nothing ever happened to it. And, it was sort of a statement to himself. He'd become successful enough to afford it, but now he'd become self-assured enough to no longer need it.

Jeff watched the buyer drive away the sports car. Then he went back into his house to get the keys for his SUV. He'd promised his mom that he'd stop by the arts and crafts fair that was going on this weekend. His mom and Mrs. Waters had purchased booth space, and from what he'd heard so far, sales were going well. Jeff was happy for both of them.

Jeff started the engine and backed out of his driveway. He adjusted the radio to a new station, then pulled onto the street. It was a warm spring Saturday, the sky blue, the air fresh, and Jeff was determined to make this a good day.

His mom had told him that Mrs. Waters had continued to purge her junk and that she'd had some colossal conversation with her ex-husband. Jeff hated to always get information second-hand about the Waters family, including updates on Alicia. He hadn't seen her since that day at the Main Street Café, and that had been more than a month ago. But he'd determined that she'd have to come to him if she wanted to ever be friends again. Meanwhile, he'd concentrate on developing his real estate business and rebuild from the mistakes his cousin had brought in.

On a personal level, he'd decided not to date for a while. He didn't have an exact time limit in place, but he made it a general practice not to go to parties and get-togethers his friends might invite him to.

Jeff pulled into the parking lot of the arts and crafts fair. He was surprised at the number of cars, but then again it was Saturday. He paid the small entrance fee, then looked around for his mom's booth.

"Jeff!" someone called out.

He turned to see his friend Grant Shelton—the person he'd left a message with about doing some repair work when he'd first started spending time with Alicia.

"It's been a while," Grant said. "Did you ever get my message after you called me a couple of months ago?"

"Yeah, sorry I didn't call you back," Jeff said. "It turns out I didn't need your help after all.

"No worries," Grant said. "Looks like you've been busy though. I've seen your realtor signs up everywhere."

Jeff laughed. "Just keeping busy. What about you?" "The same old thing—working nonstop, it seems."

A woman came up to them and slipped her hand into Grant's.

Jeff couldn't be more surprised. Grant had always sworn

off any guys-get-togethers, especially if it involved women. He had a kid from his first marriage, which had been a rocky one, so he frequently used the dad card to get out of invitations.

"Maurie, do you remember Jeff?" Grant asked.

"I think so," she said in a slow voice, tilting her head to study him.

Jeff didn't recognize the woman. She was pretty with dark, curly hair, and green eyes. And it seemed Grant liked her a lot. That was good news in Jeff's book; it meant his friend might have actually found some happiness in his life after his cruddy divorce.

"Jeff, this is Maurie Ledbetter," Grant said. "She used to live down the street from me, but she was mostly home-schooled."

"Okay," Jeff said, holding out his hand and shaking Maurie's. "Nice to see you."

"Well, we'd better get going," Grant said. "We're picking up Trent from his mom."

Jeff was definitely going to call Grant after this to find out more details about what was going on with this new woman. "Great, we'll need to catch up sometime."

"See you later, man," Grant said, pulling Maurie along with him.

Jeff watched the couple walk away. They seemed to be in sync, and he wondered if he'd ever have that.

He turned to survey the various booths; then he started to walk through them, thinking he might return to the booth with western sculptures. A couple of minutes later, he found his mom's booth. Several women were crowded around it, and his mom and Mrs. Waters were busy answering questions and displaying jewelry. When his mom looked his way, Jeff waved. She smiled and mouthed, "Come back in a little bit."

So Jeff moved away, intent on returning to the western

sculpture booth, when he bumped into a woman. "Sorry," he said, reaching out to steady the woman. Then he realized it was Alicia.

"It's okay," she said, looking up at him. Her eyes rounded. "Oh, hi."

"Hi . . . Are you okay?" he asked. She wore an olive V-neck shirt beneath a dark jacket, which made her eyes look darker than normal. He was glad to see she wore a soft, curious expression, not the skittish one she'd had when they were at the café with their moms.

"I'm fine," Alicia said. "Looks like this place is busy—a good thing for our moms."

"Yeah." Jeff shoved his hands in his pockets. The conversation was definitely awkward, but he couldn't come up with anything better to say or any question to ask to prolong their interaction.

But Alicia hadn't made her excuses and left either.

The smallest hope grew inside Jeff, but he tamped it down. It was only a coincidence that they'd run into each other.

"So, how have you been doing?" Alicia asked.

She was still standing in front of him, and she was asking him questions. Jeff blinked. "Busy," he said. Then he gave a self-deprecating laugh. "Don't you hate it when people say that? I mean, it's like they're saying they're busier and more important than the person they're talking to."

"True," Alicia said with a nod. A small smile had turned up her pale red lips.

Jeff wondered if she was wearing lip gloss.

"Maybe it's just a brush off, like when someone says 'fine.'" She slipped her hands into her jeans pockets, and Jeff couldn't help but notice how well her jeans fit her curves.

"I just saw Grant Shelton—remember him?" Jeff asked. "We both talked about how busy we are."

Alicia gave a small laugh, and Jeff's heart tripped.

"Grant was a couple of years older than us, right?" she asked. "One of those all-state athlete guys?"

"Yeah, I think he played a few sports."

Alicia glanced away for a split second. Was she done speaking to him? Did she wish that they hadn't run into each other? "So what's Grant up to? Besides being busy."

Jeff could answer these questions. "He's dating someone. He went through a divorce, you know, and has a kid."

Alicia nodded. "Yeah, I think I remember that. Who's he dating?"

"Maurie someone . . . Do you know her?"

"I don't think so," she said. "What about you?"

"Do I know Maurie?"

"No, are you dating someone?"

Jeff blinked. He was totally unprepared for this question from Alicia. That small bit of hope returned. "I'm not." He saw her swallow.

"No Paige?"

"Definitely no Paige," he said. "And I don't think I'll be dating for a while."

Her brows shot up. "Oh, really? Why not?"

It was Jeff's turn to swallow, and he couldn't believe he was about to say this. "Because it's going to be hard to find a woman who will compare to you."

Alicia's face pinked, and one side of her mouth lifted. She didn't act completely surprised at his comment, only pleased.

His hope grew.

And she still wasn't trying to walk away.

"My mom said the hot cocoa was really good here," she said. "And the giant cinnamon rolls."

Jeff grinned. "Cinnamon rolls, huh? Should we go see if your mom's right?"

Alicia gave a tiny shrug, but her smile had grown.

So they walked together toward the food trucks. Everything smelled and looked delicious, Jeff decided. Maybe he was just really hungry, but he would have eaten whatever Alicia wanted if it meant spending more time with her. He knew he shouldn't be letting himself have this much hope. She'd been pretty adamant about *not* being friends. So he wasn't quite sure what was going on right now; but he wasn't going to question it at this point.

While they stood in line behind a frazzled young mom with two small kids, Alicia nudged his arm. "I'm paying, just so you know."

"I can pay," Jeff said.

"If anyone owes anyone anything, it's *me* who owes *you*." She placed a hand on his chest when he tried to argue. "You brought your mom into my mom's life. And she's made miraculous changes. I'll never be able to thank you for that, so let me buy you a cinnamon roll."

Jeff was only thinking about how her hand was on his chest. Through his clothing, he could feel the warmth from the pressure of her palm. Could she feel how hard his heart was thumping? He nodded. "Okay, but only if you insist."

Her laugh was light. "I insist."

She dropped her hand and turned forward again as if she hadn't just shifted his entire world.

The young mom with the kids placed her order, then Alicia stepped up and ordered two cinnamon rolls and two hot cocoas. They sat at the end of a long picnic table, while another group of people occupied the other end.

"How's the real estate market?" she asked after they settled on their seats.

"Overall, it's been great for me," he said. "Now that I've been in business for a while, I get a lot of personal referrals from previous clients. Also, with the court case over, I'm way more focused on what I need to be."

"Did your cousin ever counter-sue?" she asked, then took a sip of her hot chocolate.

"Not yet," he said. "Dawson says the longer Kyle waits, the harder it will be for him to build a case." He shrugged. "Not that he really has a case anyway."

"I'm glad." Alicia cut into her cinnamon roll and took a bite. The rolls were so gooey with frosting that they took a fork and knife to eat.

"How's your job going?" he asked, after taking a bite of his own roll. It was as delicious as it smelled.

Alicia exhaled. "It's the same as always. Pretty boring, actually. No exciting confrontations with ex-girlfriends lately."

Jeff groaned. "I can't believe Paige did that."

"What ever happened to her?" she asked in a casual tone, but Jeff could tell she was genuinely curious.

"I haven't heard from her since the day I threatened to file a restraining order against her."

Alicia's mouth fell open. "You didn't."

"I did," Jeff said. "Dawson recommended bringing it up. It worked. She dropped all contact."

"I keep expecting that picture she took of me to show up on social media somewhere as a death threat meme."

"Hopefully, she's smarter than that," Jeff said. "I just don't know why I even started dating Paige in the first place."

Alicia laughed.

"What's so funny?"

"Paige is model gorgeous. I mean, every man probably

wants to date her," Alicia said. "And the ones who don't, fantasize about dating her."

Jeff took a sip of his own hot chocolate. It was the perfect temperature now. "Those men are wasting their time, just like I was. I'm not exactly proud of some of my decisions. But I'm working to make changes."

This seemed to interest Alicia. "What changes?"

He pulled out his phone and showed her the picture of his Lamborghini with its new owner. "This is Eric—the man I just sold my car to this morning."

Alicia stared. "You *sold* it? Why?"

"Like I said, I'm making some changes." Jeff smiled at her surprised expression. "Hey, do you want to check out the booth with western sculptures with me?"

"Okay," Alicia said, with no hesitation at all.

That was good enough for Jeff.

Twenty-one

Alicia didn't want to lead Jeff on, yet she wanted to lead him on . . . straight into accepting her apology. But the arts and crafts fair wasn't exactly a private place to explain how she'd made a mistake. She had needed some time to herself to figure out if she was willing to risk her heart, if she was willing to accept Jeff into her life—past, present, and future Jeff.

They walked to a booth that displayed small sculptures of horses and cowboys and wolves, and other creatures. Some of them were cast in bronze, and Alicia could admit that the sculptor was talented.

"What about this one?" Jeff asked, pointing to a pair of horses, both of them frozen mid-stride.

Alicia bent close. The detail was remarkable, and she could imagine the horses running across a vast plain, manes blowing in the wind, with the setting sun a backdrop. "I like it," she said. Then she looked at the price tag. "Three hundred fifty dollars? Wow."

"It's original art," Jeff said. "And I like it, and since I have my own house, no one else can tell me how to decorate it."

Alicia smiled. "Oh, so that's how it is. Do you have a cowboy western theme in your home?"

"Not exactly," he said, his blue eyes filled with amusement.

"Well, I have no problem with you getting this horse sculpture. Even if it is three-fifty."

Jeff nodded. "Thanks. I did make a profit on the Lamborghini."

"You really don't have to justify anything to me," she said, touching his arm and squeezing. She kept doing this—touching him—although Jeff hadn't seemed to mind. She dropped her hand.

"Okay, that's good," Jeff said with a wink. "Do you want one?"

"A sculpture?" Alicia asked, incredulous. "No, I'm good. I'm not really in the market for a sculpture, and I'm afraid it's a little out of my price range."

Jeff rotated the sculpture of the horses. "It would be a gift."

She folded her arms. Sometimes Jeff was kind of outrageous. "No, I can't accept such an expensive gift from you."

Jeff met her eyes. "You haven't even looked at all of them."

Alicia laughed off his comment, although she was feeling plenty warm inside. Jeff was being a lot more friendly and receptive than she'd expected. This made her think that he would forgive her, or had already. "I don't need to. I just know I don't want one."

"Fair enough," he said, holding her gaze a moment longer. Then he walked over to the sales person and made arrangements to purchase the sculpture. Moments later, it was bubble-wrapped and nestled in a thick plastic bag.

When he returned to Alicia's side, he said, "Do you want to look at anything else?"

She shrugged. "Not especially. I came to see my mom, but not really to shop."

"Same here." Jeff held up his purchase.

They both laughed.

"Remember the rock necklace I gave you the summer before high school?" he suddenly said.

"The one you made from that green rock we found?" Alicia said in a slow voice.

"Yeah, and then you lost it."

Alicia felt her face heat. "Don't remind me. I felt terrible."

"I think we can get rid of that guilt," Jeff said with a sly look.

"How?"

"There's a booth over there that sells rock jewelry," he said. "I saw it on the way over to our moms' booth."

"Really?" Alicia said. "They're probably not as good as the one you made for me."

"Of course not." He laughed. "Let's go check it out."

Alicia walked with him over to another booth. The jewelry was clunky, but unique. Nothing she'd normally wear, but if Jeff was so insistent . . .

"What do you think of this?" He held up a necklace made with a black ribbon, from which dangled a green stone wrapped in silver prongs.

Alicia moved to where he was standing. "It looks pretty flimsy."

Jeff shrugged. "It's five bucks, so not really a huge loss if it breaks." His gaze searched hers. "It's pretty, though, right?"

"I like it," Alicia said.

He grinned. "Let's see what it looks like."

Before she could say anything, he moved behind her and slipped the necklace around her neck.

She touched the rock where it nestled against the hollow of her neck. It was more of a choker necklace than anything. "How does it look?" She turned to face him, realizing that he was still standing very close.

"Beautiful," he said, but he wasn't looking at the necklace when he spoke.

Jeff bought the necklace without taking it off again. He also tried to buy her a matching bracelet too, but Alicia said she didn't wear bracelets. Too much jingling. Jeff found that funny.

As they walked away from the booth, silence fell between them. Alicia wanted to find a way to tell him she was sorry for all she'd said to him before, but maybe he understood? He had just bought her a necklace, and he wasn't exactly shying away from her.

"Do you want to help me find a place for my new sculpture?" he asked, looking over at her.

"At your house?" she asked, her pulse drumming just a little harder.

"I think it would look better there than at my office."

Alicia hesitated. He wanted her to come to his house. Frankly, she was interested in seeing it—where he spent his nights and probably most of his weekends.

"All right," she said. "Do you need to tell your mom or anything?"

"Nah," Jeff said. "I'll call her later. It looks like they've stayed busy the whole time I've been here."

Alicia sighed. "I'm so glad they're so successful."

They'd made it to the parking lot, and Alicia spotted his SUV. Her car was only a couple of rows away.

"I'll follow you," she told him.

He didn't seem surprised. "That sounds great."

They parted ways, and as Alicia climbed into her car, then pulled out to follow him, she hoped this was a good decision. It would at least give her some privacy to apologize. That thought made her feel nervous all over again, but she was determined to do it. She had to address the elephant in the room.

She followed Jeff as he left the fair grounds and drove past the ski resort turnoff. Once they turned onto Oak Street, she knew he must live in the newer development her mom told her was built about three years ago. They passed several houses and made a couple more turns. The houses grew farther and farther apart as the lots grew bigger. Finally, Jeff pulled up to a house that was at the end of a street. It had a secluded feel, since it was on at least an acre lot. Past the front yard rose a hillside of trees, which eventually extended into more mountainous property.

By the position of his house, she guessed that from his backyard he had a good view of the mountains. The garage door opened as Jeff drove up the driveway. She was about to park on the road when Jeff got out of his SUV and motioned for her to park in the driveway. So Alicia pulled into the driveway.

She turned off the ignition and took a deep breath. Jeff was waiting for her, and she knew she had to talk to him and apologize. This was the moment. He smiled as she climbed out of the car. "Nice place," she said. "It's kind of like your own little neighborhood."

His eyebrows lifted. "It's quiet. My closest neighbor lives overseas most of the year." He led the way through the garage, carrying his wrapped sculpture. As they entered the house, he flipped on lights.

The interior reminded her of a modern cabin. Knotty wood door frames, jewel-toned rugs, and leather furniture. And it was so . . . clean. Almost sparse.

She stood in the front room and looked out the tall windows that overlooked the front yard and street. "The architecture is beautiful. And everything is so clean."

"Clean?" Jeff said. "I guess that what happens with only one person living here." He started to rip off the bubble wrap from the sculpture.

Alicia watched him walk to the fireplace mantle. In the center was an old clock that looked as if it had seen better days. "This was my grandpa's," Jeff said, moving the clock to one end of the mantle. Then he put the statue in the center of the mantle.

Stepping back, he said, "What do you think?"

"It looks good there and goes with the theme of the room." Alicia folded her arms against the slight chill of the room.

"My grandpa would have liked it," Jeff said. "It's fitting that the sculpture shares the mantle with the clock."

"I remember meeting your grandpa a few times," Alicia said. "When did he pass away?"

Jeff turned to her. "About five years now. I can't believe it's been that long." He frowned. "Are you cold?"

She didn't really want to admit she was, since she wouldn't be staying long anyway. "Not really."

Jeff smirked and moved to turn on the fireplace switch. Orange gas flames leapt up instantly in the dark space. "Do you want a tour?"

"Sure," Alicia said. She was stalling with her apology, and she knew it.

"The kitchen's the second-best part of this place," he said, leading the way and turning on more light.

The kitchen's knotty wood cupboards offset the thick slab of granite that made up the countertops. It looked like a kitchen out of a magazine. "It's beautiful. A gourmet chef could be happy in here."

Jeff pointed upward to the chef's rack over the large square island. "I don't have the traditional hanging pots and pans, but it will be a selling point if I ever move."

Alicia walked about the kitchen. "Do you not keep anything on the counters? Like a bag of chips or a loaf of bread?"

Leaning on the island and watching her, Jeff said, "I have so much room in the cupboards. And the pantry is huge."

Alicia stopped and faced him. "I guess I'm used to tons of clutter. Although she's been a lot better with the help of your mom, and I've continued to purge when I can."

"My mom said they've cleaned out a bunch of stuff together."

"Yeah," she said. "You probably wouldn't recognize that place." This of course brought up her memory of them kissing in the hallway, then her bedroom. If only he wouldn't look at her like he was paying attention to her every move.

"I'm glad your mom is doing better," he said. "Ironically, their friendship has been great for my mom too. I think my parents drive each other a little batty with my dad's retirement."

"I can imagine," Alicia said with a smile. "I mean, there's only so much time you can spend with one person and not start to get bugged by their quirks."

Jeff tilted his head, his expression amused. "Like how you tell me you're not cold when you really are."

"And like how you always try to help me, even when I tell you not to," Alicia said.

Jeff's brows raised, and he walked around the counter so

they were only a few feet apart. "And how your first response to me is always *no*."

Alicia's lips quirked. "And how you told me that Dawson owed you a favor and there was no charge on my mom's case."

"There wasn't."

Alicia rolled her eyes and leaned against the counter. "So what favor did you do for Dawson?"

"Lawyers don't have a lot of friends," he said with a smirk. "So I fill in from time to time."

"So you're like a rent-a-friend?"

Jeff laughed. "He's actually a good guy, despite his larger-than-life personality."

"I guess it works in the courtroom."

He nodded. "Hey, I know we ate those cinnamon rolls, but that's not exactly a meal or anything. What do you think about ordering pizza?"

"And pizza is a *meal*?"

Jeff grinned and walked to the fridge. Opening the freezer door, he said, "Otherwise, our choices are microwave teriyaki bowls, frozen chicken pot pies, brownie fudge ice cream, or pizza rolls. There are a couple of unidentifiable lumps in some Ziplock freezer bags. They're probably from my mom."

"I think you should order pizza," Alicia said. "Then maybe the ice cream for dessert?"

"Deal."

He pulled out his phone, but before he called, Alicia said, "Wait."

Jeff looked up. "You want the teriyaki bowl?"

"No," she said. "Pizza's fine, but . . . I owe you an apology."

Jeff just watched her.

"I was pretty harsh the last time we talked, after you laid everything out for me," she said in a rush. "I know I said I didn't even want to be friends, which was really immature of me. We were friends for a long time, and there's no reason we can't be friends again. It's just that I was hurt, as you know, and then we were spending time together. And I was confused half the time. Then we kissed, and I felt vulnerable all over again. I couldn't think straight. Not with everything going on with my mom, and your mom suddenly being around her all of the time—"

"Alicia," Jeff said, crossing to her and grasping her hands. "Apology accepted."

She exhaled and stared up at him. "Just like that?" He was still holding her hands, and her heart was pounding like mad.

"Just like that," he said, his blue eyes steady on hers.

He leaned toward her, and for a moment, she thought . . . Then he released her hands and said, "What kind of pizza? Do you still like Hawaiian?"

The nervous knot in her stomach had lessened, only to be replaced by a riot of butterflies. He was standing maybe two feet away from her, and she could only think about touching him again.

"Maybe pepperoni?" Jeff asked, giving her a weird look—as if he was wondering why she was suddenly mute.

Alicia blinked. "I'm not picky."

Jeff raised a brow, as if he didn't believe her. He called in the pizza, one large, half pepperoni and half Hawaiian.

Alicia knew she had to put some distance between them, or she might make a fool of herself. How did she ever think she could just be friends with Jeff when every part of her wanted to wrap her arms about him and never let go?

She had to distract herself, so she said, "How about a tour of your house?"

Twenty-two

Jeff paid the pizza delivery kid, then thanked him. The box was still warm, so that was a good sign. When he entered the kitchen again, Alicia was sitting on a stool at the island. It was both strange and amazing to have her in his house. He'd wondered if she'd ever see it—especially after their no-contact policy.

He wasn't sure exactly what had changed over the past few weeks, but he had no problem accepting Alicia's apology. He sensed their moms might have something to do with her change of heart. Or maybe she would have eventually changed her mind anyway. Whatever it was, Jeff was grateful. He just worried that with her mom getting better, Alicia might move and leave Pine Valley.

Alicia was the woman he wanted in his life, had always wanted in his life. He just had to figure out a way to get her to trust him once and for all, and in the process not scare her off. So, they'd just be friends. They'd do things on her terms. Her pace. Whatever that might be.

He set the pizza on the counter. "Hot and ready," he said, opening the box. "They even sent napkins."

Alicia had found some plates and two water bottles.

"Looks good," Alicia said. She pulled out one of the Hawaiian slices and took a bite.

"How is it?" Jeff asked, setting two slices of pepperoni on his plate.

"Great," Alicia mumbled. "Really great. Good choice."

Jeff smiled and settled on the stool next to her. He could have sat one stool away, but he figured he'd take his chances.

Alicia didn't seem to mind, at least that he could tell.

"So," Alicia said. "My mom has been talking about selling the house and getting into a condo—at one of those active retirement communities."

Jeff drank from his water bottle. "Really?" What did this mean for Alicia? Would she move away? "That's kind of a big deal."

"Yeah, tell me about it," she said. "My mom and dad had some big talk a couple of weeks ago, and my mom then spent two hours on a call with the therapist. The outcome of it all is that my mom is still carrying a lot of baggage and guilt from the divorce. Moving will be a big step in the healing process."

"That makes sense," he said, casting her a sidelong glance. "If your mom sells the house and moves, what does that mean for you?"

"I don't know," Alicia said, then took her own drink of water. "I mean, I thought about buying the house, but I don't really have enough for a down payment, plus it needs some work. Gwen said I can move in with her—she has a roommate who is moving in the summer. So I might end up on the couch for a little while, depending on how quickly everything happens. Otherwise, I could stay at my mom's new place until

I figure things out. But that would be weird, you know. Living in a retirement community."

"That would be weird," he agreed.

She rose to clear her plate. Apparently she was going to eat only one slice of pizza. "Want some ice cream?"

"Sure." Jeff finished off his second slice while he watched her scoop up the brownie fudge ice cream. Two scoops for her, three for him.

"You remembered," he said.

"That you're a three-scoop kind of guy?" Alicia said with a smile. She slid the bowl and spoon across the island toward him. "You're kind of predictable that way."

"You think so?" Jeff said. "I'll take that as a compliment."

She laughed, then took a bite of her ice cream. She closed her eyes for a moment as she savored it. Jeff couldn't help but watch her. When she opened her eyes, her cheeks flushed as she caught him staring.

"Good?" he teased.

"Yep." She took another bite of the ice cream, but this time she didn't close her eyes. "Since you're Mr. Realtor Guy, what are the chances of my mom making a decent sale on the house? She doesn't want to put in a lot of money to fix it up. Is that going to hurt her?"

"Not really," Jeff said. "Some things might have to be fixed before it goes on the market, but we can also make it clear that the house price is for the 'as-is' condition, and maybe even advertise it as a fixer upper."

Alicia nodded. "That sounds good. What's your realtor's commission, and what do you think the house will sell for?"

"You want to talk business?" Jeff teased.

She gave him a half-smile. "I do."

"All right, let me get my laptop." He finished off his ice cream, then went to the main floor office. He was going to bring it into the kitchen, but Alicia had followed him.

She perched on the edge of his desk while he pulled up the MLS listings website. He typed in the address of the street, and the buying and selling history of each house popped up. "We have to look at comps to determine our ballpark figure. To get a real number, we'd need to bring in an inspector."

"Look," Jeff continued, pointing to a listing from a couple of months back. "This sold in two weeks—which is great for winter. You could probably ask for about the same price, since your lot is larger."

"Really?" Alicia said, leaning over to study the computer screen.

It wasn't fair that she smelled so good. Like brownie fudge ice cream. Jeff scooted his office chair back and stood. "You can sit down if you want."

"It's okay," she said. "I just want an estimate to tell my mom. She asked me what I thought about hiring you."

Jeff shoved his hands in his pockets, because it was the best course of action when standing so close to Alicia. "And what did you say?"

"I told her you were the best in town," she said with a smile.

He shrugged. "I am pretty good."

"Ha. Ha."

They didn't speak for a moment. "So, uh, I was thinking that if you end up without a place to stay," he started, "I've got two extra bedrooms upstairs. It would be like your own apartment."

Alicia's mouth opened for a moment, then closed. "I don't think so, but I appreciate the offer. It's good to have friends who want to help."

Jeff should have known she'd turn him down. Of course she would. "I have a hot tub, too. Great view of the mountains. A gourmet chef's dream kitchen."

"I know," Alicia said. "Your house is amazing, and I'm sure you'd be a great roommate."

"The best."

She sighed. "That would be the problem though."

"Being a good roommate?" he asked. "I clean up after myself. We could put together a laundry rotation schedule."

"No, that's not what I mean." She straightened from where she had perched on the desk. "People would assume . . ."

He waited for her to finish, although he knew what she was getting at. When she merely stared at him, he said, "Would that be so bad?"

"No," she whispered. She cleared her throat. "I just don't want to mess anything up. I like it when we're friends."

"I do too." Jeff pulled his hands from his pockets and raised his hands. "But I wouldn't complain if we decided to be more than friends."

Alicia merely looked at him. He couldn't read her expression, and he wished he could, so he'd know whether he should kiss her. Because that was what he really wanted to do.

"I can't trust myself," she said, and her eyes filled with tears. "And I don't want to hurt you."

"Hey, what's wrong?" Jeff said, wondering what he'd said to make her want to cry.

She turned from him but didn't leave the room. Wiping at her eyes, she took a deep breath. "I like you more than as a friend, Jeff." She glanced at him, then away again. "Are you happy now?"

Jeff moved so that he was standing in front of her. "I won't be happy if liking me makes you feel miserable."

"I'm not miserable," she said, wiping at her cheeks again. "That's not why I'm crying."

He handed her a Kleenex from the box on his desk. She took it, a sheepish expression on her face. "Thanks. I don't know why I cry so much around you."

"Do you want to sit down and talk?" he asked. "Eat more pizza? Get in the hot tub?"

Her lips twitched. "No."

"What do you want, Alicia?" he asked, grabbing her free hand. "I'll find a way to get it for you."

She closed her eyes for a second. And when she opened them, she looked more clear-eyed. "I want you, Jeff."

He stared at her, his heart thumping. "I can live with that."

She smiled through her tears, and then she stepped toward him and wrapped her arms about his waist. He pulled her close. It was remarkable that with her in his arms, he felt as if anything that had ever worried him before now didn't matter. He rubbed her back and felt her relax against him.

"But I'm not moving in with you," she said against his chest.

"I know," Jeff said, chuckling.

"I am really sorry." She pulled slightly away so she could look at him. "You confessed your feelings, and I basically stomped on your heart."

He lifted his hand and smoothed back her hair. "I know. But I forgive you."

"Good," she said, but then her brows furrowed. "You haven't changed your mind about liking me, have you?"

Jeff moved his fingers to trail along her neck, then behind her head. "That will never change. But I am wondering if I kiss you, will that scare you off again?"

He thought she might laugh, but her expression was serious when she said, "No."

Jeff smiled. Then just before he kissed her, he whispered, "I'll take good care of your heart, I promise." He pressed his mouth against hers and tasted her sweetness, which still had a trace of chocolate.

She rested her hands on his chest and kissed him back. He kissed her slowly as the warmth from her return kisses spread through him. Her body seemed to melt against his, and he wasn't sure where he ended and she began.

Alicia's hands moved over his shoulders. Then her fingers curled into his hair. She pulled him with her as she moved back against the desk, anchoring them both against it. Jeff knew this kiss was different than their first kiss. She was opening herself up to him, drawing him in, giving up a part of her heart. He intensified his kisses, and when she responded, he felt as if he was floating in a whirl of sensations.

He didn't know if this was the beginning of something amazing; he could only hope. She had said she wanted him, and that was good enough for him right now. He lifted his head to catch his breath, and she met his gaze. The sight of her haze-filled eyes and swollen lips only made him want to kiss her more.

"You're beautiful, Alicia," he whispered.

She smiled, and he bent forward and trailed a line of kisses along her neck. She gave a small moan and arched her neck.

Then Jeff was tasting her mouth again, and she kissed him back just as deeply. He felt as if he'd been waiting ten years for this, or more than ten years. He lifted her thighs, and she wrapped her legs around his waist as he sat her on top of the desk. Some items might have scattered to the ground, but Jeff didn't really care. He was holding Alicia in his arms, and she was kissing him.

"Jeff," she whispered against his mouth.

"Hmm?" He didn't want to talk.

"I think I heard a car door shut," she said.

He lifted his head. "What?"

Alicia ran her hands down his chest, then drew away. "Are you expecting company?"

"No," he said. Then he remembered. "My mom." He stepped back, running a hand through his hair, then tucking in a part of his shirt that had come untucked. "She said she might come over after—"

"Jeff?" his mom's voice rang out clearly, as if she was in the next room. Which she apparently was.

Alicia was frantically trying to smooth down her hair and straighten her clothing. Jeff might have laughed if his mom wasn't within hearing distance. "I'm in the office."

"I saw Alicia's car outside," his mom continued, her voice getting closer.

And then she stood in the doorway.

Jeff was sitting in the office chair, the laptop open, and Alicia was leaning a hip against the desk, in a total casual pose.

"Ah, you are here," his mom said to Alicia.

"Hi, Mrs. Finch," Alicia said, in a perfectly innocent voice.

How did she do that?

"Jeff's going to be my mom's realtor," Alicia continued, "so he's showing me some comps."

Jeff watched his mom's eyebrows lift just barely. Did she suspect?

"That's great," his mom said. "I brought back the book stands you let me borrow for the booth and was going to see if you wanted to get something to eat, but it looks like you ordered pizza?" The interest in her voice was unmistakable.

184

"Yeah, we got talking, and I was hungry, so—" Jeff started.

"Do you want some pizza?" Alicia cut in. "I can warm some up for you."

"No, that's all right," his mom said, then looked back at Jeff, her eyes lively. "Dad might be waiting for me."

"Okay, I'll grab the book stands from your car," Jeff said, rising from the chair and practically ushering his mom out the door.

Once they were outside, his mom turned on him. "What's going on between the two of you?" she whispered loudly, as if Alicia could hear them from inside the house.

"Her mom's selling their house," he said. "Alicia wants me to be the realtor. We were just looking at—"

"I got that much," his mom said, eyeing him. "Did I interrupt something else?"

"No." Jeff didn't want to embarrass Alicia by telling his mom that she *had* interrupted something.

She turned and opened the trunk of her car, clearly not believing him.

Jeff lifted out the two metal stands his mom had borrowed. "How did the day end up at the fair?"

"Really great," she said. "We'll have a decent profit, but you know I don't really do it for money. I like staying busy."

"Yep," he said. "If you need to borrow these again, let me know."

"I will," she said. "Thanks again, and I want to know what's going on with Alicia when you're ready to tell me."

"Mom—"

She shooed him away. "Bye, Jeff. Have a nice evening." She climbed into her car and backed out of the driveway.

He watched her drive down the road. The daylight had faded, and the sun was setting in a pink and orange riot of colors, splashing across the sky. It was too beautiful not to share with Alicia. Jeff turned back to the house and carried the book stands inside.

Alicia was in the kitchen, cleaning up the rest of their meal. "Hey," she said when he came in. "What did you tell her?"

"Nothing." He set the book stands next to the island. "Although she can probably guess. My mom is kind of smart that way."

Alicia smiled, but it was strained.

He walked around the island to where she was standing and took her hand. "Come here, I want to show you something." She let him lead her through the house, to the sliding glass doors that overlooked the backyard. The snow on the mountain was bathed in golds and pinks, soaking up the rays of the setting sun.

"Wow, it's beautiful," she breathed.

"Um hm." Jeff slipped his arms around her waist from behind, then rested his chin on her shoulder.

She leaned back against him and exhaled. "You really didn't tell your mom?"

"I didn't want you to feel awkward, so I kept to our story."

"Okay," she said. "I don't mind telling our parents, just not like two minutes after we were . . . you know."

Jeff smiled and inhaled the scent of her hair. Strawberries. "We'll tell them whenever you're ready. Sneaking around might be kind of fun, though."

She laughed and turned to face him. She looped her arms about his neck. "Remember what you were doing before your mom interrupted?"

He grinned. "I do."

She raised up on her toes and brought her face to within an inch of his, closing her eyes. "Do that again."

Twenty-three

Two Months Later

"It looks great," Alicia told her mom.

Her mom stepped back from the wall where she'd hung a row of framed pictures of pressed wildflowers. Her own artwork. It had taken them all week to get moved into her mom's new condo, and now Alicia had to finish cleaning out their old house before the new owners moved in.

Even though her mom had encouraged her to stay in the extra bedroom at the condo, Alicia had decided to rent a room in Gwen's place. Jeff kept offering his place as well, but Alicia wasn't about to commit to him that much . . . unless they were married. But she wasn't about to tell Jeff that. She didn't want to force him into anything.

"Thanks for all of your help," her mom said, looping an arm about Alicia's shoulders.

The affection from her mom was definitely a new thing.

And Alicia wasn't complaining. Her mom had come a long way since last summer.

"Do you need anything else done?" Alicia asked.

"No, I'm good," her mom said. "Beth is coming over tonight—she says she has a house-warming gift for me."

"That sounds nice," Alicia said. She took another look around before leaving. Several boxes were still waiting to be unpacked, but most of the place was put together. The couches were cute yellow-and-white plaid, and the white walls and blue area rug made the place bright and cheery. Her mom had only kept the necessities after going through a two-week purge that took both Mrs. Finch and Alicia helping.

The compromise they'd reached was taking pictures of all of her mom's stuff, putting the pictures into photo albums, and the stuff could only be given to the assisted living center or Goodwill. Nothing could be thrown away. Alicia suspected that Goodwill had thrown away at least a third of the stuff.

Otherwise, her mom's therapist had encouraged her mom to become a collector of three things only. Her mom could buy as much of the three as she wanted, and it was no one else's business.

So, her mom had chosen decorative roosters, hot pads, and ceramic mugs to collect. It was fine with Alicia. She wasn't going to be living with her mom anyway.

As she left her mom's condo, Alicia texted Jeff. *On my way.*

His reply came as she climbed in her car. *I'll meet you there.*

Alicia smiled to herself, relishing the butterflies tumbling in her stomach every time she was with Jeff. They'd been officially in a relationship for two months now, since that day at the arts and crafts fair. But they'd only told their families about a month ago. Things had been great. Things had been better than great. Alicia knew she was in love with Jeff, and on one level it scared her to death. On another level, she'd never been happier.

By the time she reached her old house, Jeff's SUV was parked at the curb. He was sitting inside, talking on the phone. She pulled into the driveway and climbed out of her car. Jeff held up his hand, as if to say, just a minute. So Alicia walked to the porch and unlocked the door. It still had the musty smell of old junk. But now the place was all cleaned out, for the most part.

Alicia still had to do the nitty gritty, like wash down the cupboards and scrub baseboards. Jeff had told her he'd help her out today. She flipped on lights and looked around, assessing what the final things were to be done. She checked the single bathroom. It was still clean from the last time she'd cleaned it. While waiting, she walked from room to room. Her mom's bedroom had been the worst to clean out, but now it had an eerie empty feel to it. The spare bedroom, turned office, turned junk room, had also been cleaned out. Nail holes dotted the walls, and there were cobwebs in the corners.

They'd have to be cleaned off.

Next she moved to her bedroom. It was strange being in her childhood bedroom for what might be the last time. She'd gone through a lot of growing up and emotions in this room. She'd dreamed, cried, laughed, and found new purpose.

The front door opened, and Alicia stepped out into the hallway. Jeff came inside, carrying a couple bags.

"Hi." He held up the bags. "I brought cleaning supplies."

"Great," Alicia said, walking toward him. He was wearing jeans and a dark t-shirt, so he must have changed after work. His t-shirt pulled across his broad shoulders, and his forearms were already tanned with the warming weather. He set the bags on the floor and scooped her up into a hug.

"Mmm," she said against his neck, inhaling his clean spice scent. "How do you always smell so good?"

He chuckled and kissed her cheek. She turned her head so he could kiss her mouth too, which he did.

"Ready to get to work?" she asked after a moment.

He sighed. "I'm at your command," he said in a teasing voice.

"Okay, great," she said, reluctantly stepping out of his embrace, although he kept his hands loosely at her hips. "We need to finish up the spare room and the living room. I think everything else is good."

"I'll work out here if you want to do the spare room," Jeff said, his fingers tugging at the hem of her shirt. "I think it will be a lot less distracting."

"You're probably right," Alicia said. His touch and his blue eyes could easily make her forget quite a few things.

She stepped back and went through his bags. "Ah, perfect," she said, pulling out a cloth duster. "Can you get the cobwebs first?"

He laughed and took the duster. "You're going to owe me . . . something good."

She followed him to the spare room. "I'm already in debt to you."

He smiled and moved about the room, sweeping off the cobwebs. She got to work on the baseboards. Thankfully the place had been thoroughly vacuumed by Jeff's mom a couple of days ago. The carpet was still pretty scary though. Jeff moved into the next room, and the next hour went by quickly as Alicia cleaned. When she'd finished the spare room and done the baseboards of the other two bedrooms, she found Jeff in the living room, talking to someone at the door—a food delivery kid.

"You ordered takeout?" she said as he came back inside.

"Yeah, I figured we could say goodbye to this place properly."

"Are we sitting on the floor?"

He handed her the sack of food. "We're going in the backyard." He picked up another bag from the floor she hadn't noticed before, along with a thick blanket. "I brought something to sit on."

"We'll need it," Alicia said. Even though she'd done a bunch of work to get the house ready to sell, the backyard had been long neglected. The grass was cut, but it was thick with weeds, and the bushes outlining the yard probably needed to be trimmed again. At least the mature trees offered plenty of shade, blocking the late-afternoon sun.

While she held the bag of food, Jeff spread out the blanket, then pulled some other things out of the bag. Water bottles, plates, forks, napkins.

"It's like a real picnic," Alicia said with a laugh. She knelt down. "I hope you ordered chicken cashew, that's my favorite."

He grinned. "I know. And I ordered it."

She opened the containers of Chinese food, smelling each one as she went. "I must be starving. Everything looks delicious."

Jeff sat opposite of her and scooped some food from every container onto a plate. "Remember we used to play that game of double dare, or something. You had to try something new every time we ate someplace?"

"Yeah," she said. "But that was at like McDonalds, when everything pretty much tastes the same."

"Well, you have to try everything I ordered," he said, handing over her plate.

"I'm not trying this limp zucchini," Alicia said. "It looks overcooked."

Jeff shrugged. "If you don't try everything you won't get a fortune cookie."

"That's mean," she said. "Fortune cookies are my favorite."

He leaned on his side, propped up on one elbow. He picked a fortune cookie out of a plastic container, then moved the container behind him. He cracked open his cookie and ate one of the halves.

"Why do *you* get to eat the cookies first?"

"I bought the food, so I get to make the rules." Jeff spread out the strip of paper. "*Today your life will change.*"

"Hmm, sounds very mysterious," she said. She took a bite of everything that was familiar.

She noticed that Jeff didn't try everything, he mostly stuck to the sweet and sour chicken.

"Okay, here goes," she said. With Jeff watching her, she took a small bite of the limp zucchini. She made a face. "Not terrible, but I'm not eating anymore."

Jeff laughed. "I guess you earned a cookie."

"Good, I need to get the taste out of my mouth." Alicia drank from her water bottle, then held out her hand. "Cookie, please."

Jeff handed her a cookie, and she broke it open.

She popped the cookie into her mouth as she read the fortune: "*Dear Alicia: Someone will ask you a very important question today.*" She looked at Jeff. "It has my name on it."

He just looked at her, as if he wasn't surprised at all.

"Jeff, what is this?" she held up the slip of paper. Then she realized that not only did it have her name on it, but it was referring to an 'important question.' A dozen thoughts ran through her mind—the primary one being that she had just been cleaning cobwebs and baseboards for an hour. She was sweaty, her hair was a mess, and she probably didn't smell too nice.

Jeff handed her another cookie.

"What's in this one?" she asked, her pulse drumming.

Jeff just raised his brows, not answering.

Her hands shook as she broke open the cookie. When a ring tumbled out onto the blanket, she gasped. For a moment, she just stared at the diamond band. Then she looked up to see Jeff kneeling next to her and gazing at her with that look of his that made her feel like she was his whole world.

She blinked at the sudden tears in her eyes.

"Jeff," she whispered.

He picked up the ring. "Marry me, Alicia," he said. "I will always watch over you. I will always love you. And I'll always be there for you."

Her tears fell, and she took a shaky breath. "This is really fast. I—" She looked down at the ring. "I mean, I didn't expect this . . . so soon . . ."

"I didn't either," he said, "but I feel like I've been waiting a long time. And even if you want to wait, I'm okay with that too. I'll wait as long as you need. Just don't make it ten years."

Alicia's heart thumped like mad as she looked into his eyes. She felt like she was in a dream, a good dream, a very good dream. Jeff was the only man she wanted to be with, to marry, to spend the rest of her life with. Would another month make a difference? Would a year change her mind? She knew it wouldn't.

She exhaled. "I don't want to wait either."

Jeff whooped and pulled her into his arms, squeezing her tight.

Alicia laughed. "I can't breathe."

He released her just enough to kiss her hard. "I love you," he said.

"I love you, too," she whispered against his mouth. They tumbled onto the blanket together, a tangle of arms and legs as Jeff continued to kiss her.

Alicia couldn't think of a better way to spend the afternoon than kissing her fiancé. She pulled him closer, breathing in this man who had become her whole world. She ran her fingers over his shoulder then down his arm, stopping at his hand resting on her waist. "What did you do with the ring?" she asked.

He lifted his head. "What?"

"Where's the ring?"

He disentangled himself from her and sat up. "Oh, no."

She sat up, too, and they started to search the blanket and the food containers. Then she saw something sparkling in the grass a couple of feet away. She reached over and picked it up.

"Found it," she said.

Jeff moved next to her. "Maybe we should put it on where it belongs."

She smirked and held out her hand so he could slide the ring on her finger. It was beautiful and actually fit. Jeff brought her hand to his mouth and pressed a kiss on her ring finger. "That's better."

"When did you plan all of this?" she asked.

"About twelve years ago," he said. "I always thought if I was going to marry you, I'd ask you in your backyard."

She stared at him. "*Twelve years?*"

He grinned as he cleaned up the remains of the food. When he had it all shoved back into the bag, he stood and held out his hand. "It took me longer than I thought to work up the courage."

Alicia put her hand in his and let him pull her to her feet. "I'm glad you finally did."

His arms slid around her waist. "I'm a lucky man, and

I'm glad you decided I was worth the risk."

Alicia settled her hands on his shoulders. Then she kissed him, knowing in her heart that he would always be worth the risk. When she drew away, she said, "We probably shouldn't wait to tell our families *this* news."

"Probably not," Jeff said. "The sooner we tell them, the sooner we can make wedding plans. And then you can finally be my roommate."

She laughed. "That sounds good to me." They walked into her childhood home together, and Alicia knew she was finally ready to say goodbye to her old life and start a new one with Jeff.

ABOUT HEATHER B. MOORE

Heather B. Moore is a four-time *USA Today* bestselling author. She writes historical thrillers under the pen name H.B. Moore; her latest thrillers include *The Killing Curse* and *Poetic Justice*. Under the name Heather B. Moore, she writes romance and women's fiction, her newest releases include the historical romance *Love is Come*. She's also one of the coauthors of the *USA Today* bestselling series: A Timeless Romance Anthology. Heather writes speculative fiction under the pen name Jane Redd, releases include the Solstice series and *Mistress Grim*.

For book updates, sign up for Heather's email list:
hbmoore.com/contact
Website: HBMoore.com
Facebook: Fans of H. B. Moore
Blog: MyWritersLair.blogspot.com
Instagram: @authorhbmoore
Twitter: @HeatherBMoore

MORE PINE VALLEY NOVELS:

Made in United States
North Haven, CT
23 December 2022

30036433R00114